"You Really Know How To Take A Girl's Breath Away, Mr. Hollister,"

Liz said, sipping the hot, sweet Irish coffee through its crown of whipped cream.

"It's my specialty," Nathan teased, leaning forward to wipe a dollop of cream from the side of her mouth. "I like excitement in my life."

He licked the froth from his finger, and Liz shivered at the intimacy of his action. Turning from his suddenly too-intense gaze, she remembered the feel of his hard body pressed tight against hers. *Dangerous ground*, her mind warned. He wasn't making small talk easy.

"You work too much," he murmured. "You should leave some time to laugh, Liz. People who work hard need to play hard, too."

"Is that your personal philosophy?" she asked.

"What do you think?"

She thought of his reckless abandon behind the wheel of his car and of his all-out pursuit of her. He was the original man on the fast track. "But you have to slow down sometimes, don't you?" he pressed.

His handsome mouth spread into a smile as he brought her hand to his lips. "Oh, there are some things I can take very slow," he whispered.

Dear Reader:

Happy Holidays from all of us at Silhouette Books. And since it *is* the holiday season, we've planned an extra special month at Silhouette Desire. Think of it as our present to you, the readers.

To start with, we have December's *Man of the Month*, who comes in the tantalizing form of Tad Jackson in Ann Major's *Wilderness Child*. This book ties into the Children of Destiny series, but Tad's story also stands on its own. Believe me, Tad's a man you'd *love* to find under your Christmas tree.

And what would December be without a Christmas book? We have a terrific one—*Christmas Stranger* by Joan Hohl. After you've read it, I'm sure you'll understand why I say this is a truly timeless love story.

Next, don't miss book one of Celeste Hamilton's trilogy, Aunt Eugenia's Treasures. *The Diamond's Sparkle* is just the first of three priceless love stories. Look for *Ruby Fire* and *Hidden Pearl* in February and April of 1990.

Finally, some wonderful news: the *Man of the Month* will be continued through 1990! We just couldn't resist bringing you one more year of these stunning men. In the upcoming months you'll be seeing brand-new *Man of the Month* books by Elizabeth Lowell, Annette Broadrick and Diana Palmer—just to name a few. Barbara Boswell will make her Silhouette Desire debut with her man. I'll be keeping you updated....

Before I go, I want to wish all of our readers a very Happy Holiday. See you next year!

Lucia Macro
Senior Editor

CELESTE HAMILTON

THE DIAMOND'S SPARKLE

SILHOUETTE *Desire*

Published by Silhouette Books New York

America's Publisher of Contemporary Romance

SILHOUETTE BOOKS
300 East 42nd St., New York, N.Y. 10017

ISBN: 0-373-05537-4

First Silhouette Books printing December 1989

Printed in the U.S.A.

Books by Celeste Hamilton

Silhouette Special Edition

Torn Asunder #418
Silent Partner #447
A Fine Spring Rain #503
Face Value #532

Silhouette Desire

*The Diamond's Sparkle #537

*Aunt Eugenia's Treasures

CELESTE HAMILTON

began writing when she was ten years old, with the encouragement of parents who told her she could do anything she set out to do and teachers who helped her refine her talents. The broadcast media captured her interest in high school, and she graduated from the University of Tennessee with a B.S. in Communications. From there, she began writing and producing commercials at a Chattanooga, Tennessee, radio station.

Celeste began writing romances in 1985 and now works at her craft full-time. She says she "never intends to stop." Married to a policeman, she likes nothing better than spending time at home with him and their two much-loved cats, although she and her husband also enjoy traveling when their busy schedules permit. Wherever they go, however, "It's always nice to come home to East Tennessee—one of the most beautiful corners of the world."

For Mary Leamon McGuire

I can't remember when you weren't my friend.
I can't imagine life without you.
Thanks for your love and support.

One

"A pretty bunch of piranha, aren't we?"

The quiet words were followed by a throaty chuckle, and Liz Patterson turned from her perusal of the crowded hotel ballroom. She knew only one person who could so aptly label a Nashville society bash.

"Aunt Eugenia!" Liz exclaimed in delight. "I didn't think you were coming."

The elderly woman laughed again, and she submitted to a hug from her niece. "Not come? When have I ever missed an opportunity to show off, even when it's just to all these social predators?" The black sequins on her dress flashed as she straightened her shoulders.

"I should have known better," Liz murmured, stepping back to admire the effect of her great-aunt's shimmering attire. From the top of her white hair to the tips of her black slippers, Eugenia was the picture of style. Her figure was still trim enough. Her features, though stroked with aging's inevitable lines, were still delicate. Not bad for eighty, Liz approved. "You look spectacular."

"Thank you, my dear." Critically the blue eyes swept over Liz's emerald satin suit. "Didn't you wear that to my Christmas tea last year?"

"Yes, but—"

"I would have thought you'd be more festive tonight." Eugenia nodded to the colorfully attired men and women who mingled around them. "Granted, most of these people are as dull as Tennessee River mud, but I have spotted a couple of attractive men."

"I didn't come here looking for men, Aunt Eugenia. I have a date." Smiling, Liz watched the other woman's face soften in approval.

"Anyone I know?"

Liz's smile wavered. "Jim Levinson."

"Horse feathers!" Eugenia cried. "I thought for once you might be out with a *real* man."

Casting nervous glances at the crowd around her, Liz admonished her aunt, "You wouldn't say that about Jim if you really knew him—"

"I know enough to spot a wimp when I see one, thank you."

"Jim is not a wimp."

"Yes, he is." Eugenia's voice was firm. "I know it, and the good people of Tennessee know it. That's why he lost the election."

"He lost because his opponent spread a pack of vicious rumors."

"Those rumors were nonsense. No one believed Jim Levinson ever seduced anyone. He's too wishy-washy for that, and we don't need that type in Congress. The country has enough of those already. I'll never understand why you spent so much time working on his campaign." Eugenia's voice boomed over the surrounding party noise.

"Aunt Eugenia, please," Liz cautioned, noticing several heads had turned their way.

"Only a wimp would leave a woman as lovely as you standing alone at a party."

"He didn't leave me alone. He had some business to discuss with someone, and I was talking with Maggie and Paul—"

"Paul?" Eugenia echoed, snorting indelicately. "Why is it that you and Maggie O'Grady pick the least exciting men in the city to date?"

Liz jumped to her best friend's defense. "Paul is a very successful investment banker—"

"I've met him, and I imagine even his underwear drawer is arranged alphabetically," Eugenia observed dryly.

"What's wrong with being organized?"

The older woman's glance could have chilled a four-alarm blaze. "Liz, I hope to God you aren't interested in men who file their Jockey shorts."

"I get enough excitement in the courtroom," Liz said, searching the crowd for a glimpse of Jim or Maggie or anyone she knew who could distract Aunt Eugenia. At any other time Liz would be overrun with boring acquaintances. But not now—not when she needed rescuing. As much as she loved her aunt, Liz could do without another lecture on finding the perfect man.

The older woman, however, was not to be deterred. "I know life in the public defender's office is very exciting, but you can't sleep with a legal brief."

"Aunt Eugenia!"

"Oh, don't look so shocked." Eugenia's white curls bounced as she tossed her head. "I've never minced words with you about the realities of life. And the need for a man to keep your feet warm at night is just one of those realities."

Liz nodded dutifully, pretending to listen as Eugenia expounded on what had become her favorite topic—finding Liz a husband. Why the subject had become such an obsession with the woman was anyone's guess. She had not chosen matrimony for herself.

Daring and outspoken even as a young person, Eugenia had been somewhat of an embarrassment to her wealthy but conservative family. A world full of women had been bobbing their hair, wearing short skirts and doing the Charleston, and Eugenia wasn't the type to sit on the sidelines. Armed with an inheritance from her grandmother, she set off for Europe to become a photojournalist. Her career had been only a modest success, but her life had been a rich adventure. She'd ridden elephants in India, traveled in a barge down the Nile and seen Paris through dozens of springs. She'd sipped tea with queens, photographed counts and fallen in love with an assortment of suitable and unsuitable men.

But twenty years ago, she had come home to Nashville. Ten-year-old Liz and her best friends, Maggie O'Grady and Cassandra Martin, immediately became Eugenia's devoted fans. She had regaled them with stories of her many escapades. She had encouraged them to be independent and open-minded. Never had she suggested a husband was necessary to their happiness.

Never—that is—until recently.

And Liz was growing tired of this latest lecture on the merits of connubial bliss. "Aunt Eugenia," she soothed, "I'm just not ready to settle down."

"I guess I should thank God for that much." Eugenia shuddered. "If you were ready, you might end up with Jim the wimp."

"I told you, Jim's not a—"

"What you need is someone who will take your breath away. Let me see if I can show you what I mean. There was a man here earlier who reminded me of someone..." Eugenia's voice trailed away as, like a queen inspecting her retinue, she allowed her gaze to sweep the room. She frowned deeply, obviously displeased with most of what she saw. Then a nearby cluster of people shifted, and she smiled in triumph.

Liz's trepidation grew in direct proportion to the brilliant sparkle in her aunt's eyes.

"There," Eugenia whispered, pointing in an imperious manner. "Now that is what I call a man."

Praying for invisibility, Liz glanced in the direction her aunt indicated. She expected anything but the pair of hazel eyes which gazed back at her from barely ten feet away.

She recognized the eyes. The tawny hair. The winged, surprisingly dark eyebrows. The broad, confident set of the tuxedoed shoulders. She smothered a curse. "Of all the people in the room," she managed to choke out before abruptly turning her back on his far-too-interested expression.

A smile quirked the corners of Nathan Hollister's mouth as the woman in green turned away. Obviously he was the subject of a feminine conversation. Nothing wrong with that, he thought. This wasn't the first, and he hoped it wasn't the last time a woman studied him from across a room. What man wouldn't like that kind of scrutiny? Especially when the woman doing the looking was worth returning the favor.

This woman was worth more than a glance. Absolutely. Thick chestnut hair curled well past her shoulders. Emerald satin clung to her slender figure. Blue eyes. Tiny, straight nose. Red lips. Nathan had caught it all before she had looked away. He continued to gaze at her, but she didn't turn around.

The elderly woman who stood beside her was another matter entirely. She smiled and nodded at Nathan, acting for all the world as if they were good friends. Did he know her? Though he racked his brain, he couldn't come up with a name to fit the face.

Murmuring an apology to the long-winded state senator, Nathan threaded his way through the crowd. The white-haired lady's smile broadened even farther when he reached her side.

"Excuse me. Have we met?"

"I don't believe so." The woman's voice was clear and strong.

Gazing into her snapping blue eyes, Nathan was reminded sharply of the schoolteacher who had always seen through his elaborate excuses for being late to class. Then the woman smiled again, and he saw the humor that brightened her eyes. No teacher in his memory had ever revealed such a sense of fun.

"But you do seem familiar," she continued. "Your name?"

"Nathan Hollister."

"Hollister?" she repeated. "Any relation to Rupert Hollister of Memphis?"

"My grandfather," Nathan said proudly.

"Of course, of course, I should have known. You look just as Rupert did years ago. When he and I were much younger." She winked and held out her hands. Nathan took them in his. "I'm Eugenia Davis, an old friend of your grandfather's. It's so very nice to meet you."

Nathan laughed in delight at her openness. Gently squeezing her frail fingers with his own, he filled her in on his grandfather's latest exploits. From the way she talked, he got the distinct impression she had been more than his grandfather's "friend." He could understand why. Like his grandson, Rupert Hollister had an appreciation for beauty, and Eugenia Davis must have been gorgeous in her prime.

"And this is my grandniece, Liz Patterson," she said, nodding at the young woman who stood beside her.

Dropping Eugenia's hands, Nathan watched her companion make a reluctant turn from the crowd. She frowned at her aunt, and in the second before she acknowledged his presence, he had time to appreciate the similarity in looks between the two women.

Then Liz's blue-eyed gaze flashed up to meet his. Not teasing like her aunt's, this gaze was sharp enough to cut through the poise of a less confident man.

"You should have asked me earlier, Aunt Eugenia," she said, without greeting Nathan even though she stared at him. "I could have told you Mr. Hollister's name."

"Do we know each other?" Though he felt compelled to ask the question, Nathan doubted he would have forgotten someone as lovely as Liz.

Liz continued, "I believe it was Mr. Hollister's public relations firm that directed the campaign of our new Congressman, Hugo Mantooth."

"Oh, dear," Eugenia murmured.

Nathan glanced at her, puzzled.

Eugenia hastened to explain. "Liz was a staunch supporter of Mr. Mantooth's opponent."

"As a matter of fact, I'm here with Jim Levinson tonight," Liz said, finally directing a remark to Nathan.

He hesitated a moment, noting the challenge in her eyes. Evidently Ms. Patterson had a personal interest in the outcome of the recent election. That meant Nathan had nothing to lose. So, with the smoothness he'd polished to perfection, he baited her even further. "I envy Mr. Levinson." His eyes traveled slowly, meaningfully down Liz's body. "He has always been blessed with such *ardent* supporters."

His emphasis wasn't lost on Liz. Because an alleged romantic entanglement with a married campaign worker had spelled Jim's ultimate defeat, the statement hit its well-aimed mark.

"You're even more disgusting than I thought you'd be," she said dryly.

Rich laughter rolled out of Nathan. "Goodness, no one's ever called me that before."

"That's probably because the people you consort with accept disgusting as the norm."

He laughed even harder.

Eugenia stifled a giggle.

While shooting her aunt a murderous glance, Liz still managed to smile. Hollister's laughter had drawn attention, and she didn't want onlookers to think she was exchanging anything but polite conversation with him. "I'm glad you both think the character assassination of a decent, honorable man is so funny."

"Now Liz—" Eugenia began.

"You, I can forgive," Liz told her. "But since Mr. Hollister's firm started the rumors about Jim, I'm not feeling so charitable toward him." Turning on her heel but still smiling, she started to leave.

"Now wait a minute."

A firm hand closed on Liz's elbow before she could take more than a step. Struggling would only create a scene. Protesting would probably please him. Men such as this usually liked demonstrating their strength. She turned around.

Nathan left his hand on her arm a second longer than was necessary. The satin beneath his touch was smooth and warmed by her skin, a distinct contrast to the chilliness of her expression. Dropping her elbow, he stepped back. "I didn't start any rumors."

"Oh come now—"

"It was a preposterous rumor which I for one never believed. I can't imagine why anyone did."

Ignoring her aunt's smug glance, Liz tossed her head. "Well, evidently someone believed it. Or else your client wouldn't have squeaked by with a win."

"Squeaked by?" Now Nathan's laughter was derisive. "In experienced political circles, an eight-point margin of victory is not considered a *squeak*."

A flush followed the fury that streaked up Liz's body. "Are you saying I don't know what I'm talking about, Mr. Hollister?"

Thinking the color in her face only made her more beautiful, his glance locked with hers. "Maybe."

Liz made a choking sound.

Eugenia hastened to explain. "Nathan, Liz is quite experienced in political causes. She's a lawyer, and she's very active on behalf of many social issues, like housing the homeless, feeding the poor and saving the sharks—''

"The whales," Liz corrected tightly.

"Noble causes all," Nathan commented, nodding in agreement.

Liz sent him a skeptical look. "Do you really think so?"

"Of course."

"Then it's a pity your client didn't address any of those issues in his campaign."

Nathan frowned, giving the appearance of being in serious thought. "I wasn't aware that saving the whales was of major importance here in the state. Are there really whales in the Tennessee River?" he asked, all wide-eyed innocence as he turned to Eugenia.

This time Eugenia didn't giggle. She laughed, the lusty, straight-from-the-heart laughter Liz had never been able to resist. There was no point in not joining in. Nathan followed suit.

When she could manage to talk again, Eugenia hailed a waiter and procured glasses of champagne for them all. "Now isn't this much more pleasant than arguing over some silly campaign that's over and done with anyway?"

"Much nicer," Nathan agreed, admiring Liz. Laughter did even more for her peachy, glowing skin than anger.

Liz couldn't resist one last jab. "I still don't care for your sleazy, mud-slinging campaign tactics."

"Point well taken." He paused to sip his drink, gazing at her over the rim of the crystal flute. "But I want you to know that I really respect the *passion* of your commitment."

Again, there was no mistaking what word he had emphasized. Just as there was no mistaking the bold, appraising look in his hazel eyes. Or were those eyes green? Liz wondered as she gazed upward and into them.

Whatever the color, they certainly were expressive eyes, able to convey a wealth of emotion with merely a flip of his long, dark lashes. No—emotion wasn't quite the right word. The eyes were a little too cold for that. Perhaps desire was the more correct term. All that Nathan Hollister desired could probably be read in his eyes. And Liz Patterson was certain that like most men of his type, his list of desires was long and varied. She didn't care to be on it.

Eugenia coughed then, not a polite attention-getting cough but a genuine choking sound. Concerned, Liz turned to her and was surprised when Nathan's expression seemed equally worried.

"Are you all right?" he murmured.

"Oh, certainly," Eugenia replied crossly. "It's the only drawback I've found to getting older. Crowded, smoky rooms no longer agree with me."

Nathan tucked her hand in the crook of his elbow. "Then you should go." He looked at Liz. "I'd be pleased if both of you would join me for a drink somewhere else."

Liz wanted to go. But she didn't know why. Hollister wasn't the sort of man in which she was usually interested. Though she might be jumping to conclusions, she doubted he had a social conscience. And if all she'd heard about him was true, he'd betray his mother to get ahead. There was, however, something distinctly appealing about him. Perhaps it was the rumpled, little-boy tumble of his hair. Not blond but not brown, it rioted over his head like a lion's mane, longer than current styles dictated and immensely touchable.

Touchable? The very thought of running her hands through his hair popped along Liz's nerves like a string of firecrackers. She was losing her mind. She wasn't going anywhere with this man. Even in the company of her aunt. Even if she was desperately curious to know if his smooth, charming facade ever slipped.

"Well," Eugenia prompted. "Are you coming with us, Liz?" That she wanted her niece to accompany them was patently obvious.

"You've forgotten that I already have an escort for the evening," Liz returned sweetly.

Her aunt once again snorted.

"Yes, I had forgotten, too." The grin Nathan managed was closer to a smirk. "Where is the good Mr. Levinson, anyway?"

"He had business to attend to," Liz returned.

"Then I'm certain none of it is true."

Liz blinked, thrown by the abrupt statement. "What's not true?"

"The rumors about Levinson of course." With a careless gesture Nathan dusted an invisible speck of dust from his tuxedo sleeve. "If he was even half the man the rumors claimed, he never would have left someone like you standing all alone."

His words were so near an imitation of what Eugenia had said earlier that Liz gasped. Her aunt chortled merrily. Without pausing, Nathan led the elderly woman through the crowd.

But over the noise, the word *wimp* floated with unmistakable clarity back to Liz.

"Someday I'm going to choke her," Liz muttered to herself. Then she drained her remaining champagne and claimed another glass from a passing waiter.

"Okay, give. Who is he?"

The low words, spoken close to Liz's ear, caused her to jump. She turned and looked into Maggie O'Grady's laughing brown eyes. Liz purposely sipped her drink before answering.

"You heard me, Liz. Now who is he?"

"The waiter?" Liz hedged. "I haven't any idea."

"Don't be silly. Who is the hunk who disappeared with Aunt Eugenia?"

"Just some man she picked up."

Maggie's eyes widened in shock. "It's not that I don't think she's capable of picking up a man—any man—but even for Eugenia he was kind of young—"

"All right, all right—he's the grandson of one of her old beaux."

"Well, if the offspring is any way to judge, I bet this old beau was one of those she *really* fell for." The laughter which bubbled out of Maggie was high and faintly out of control. It was certainly uncharacteristic.

"You've been drinking," Liz accused, taking the champagne flute from her friend's unprotesting fingers. "And you never drink."

"I'm so bored I had to do something to liven up the party."

Liz realized she was as bored as Maggie. It wasn't a bad party. From a group nearby came a shriek of laughter. As if on cue, the band, which had been playing sedate background music, swung into an upbeat tune. Couples surged to the middle of the room to dance. All around them people were laughing, talking, flirting. But Liz and Maggie stood alone. Maybe that's the problem, Liz thought. Maybe she and Maggie spent too much time alone.

"What happened to Paul?" she asked her glum-looking friend.

"He and Jim are in some corner with about dozen other stuffed shirts discussing tax shelters."

"Stuffed shirts?" Liz was amazed. She had thought Maggie was quite taken with her handsome investment banker.

"Yeah—dull, boring stuffed shirts." Maggie reclaimed her champagne and gulped it down.

Liz heaved a gloomy sigh. "Aunt Eugenia said you and I date the dullest men in the city."

"She's right."

"But why?" Liz moaned. "We're two intelligent, interesting and attractive women, aren't we?" She eyed her friend's form-fitting blue dress. "Why is Paul in a corner with a bunch of other men when he could be dancing with a great-looking blonde?"

"Beats me. Why is Jim with him instead of with you?"

Liz stared down at her glass. "We're doing something wrong, Maggie."

"Aunt Eugenia would say it's the company we keep," Maggie offered, equally grim.

"Maybe she's right."

"Well there has to be some reason why she walked out with the best-looking man in the room and we're standing here without dance partners."

"You're right." Knowing that she could also have left with the man in question didn't do anything for Liz's spirits. Without further delay she tossed down the rest of her drink. The effervescent liquid was still tickling her throat as she looked around for another glass. "I think you've got the right idea, Maggie. Let's forget about the stuffed shirts and have some fun."

Laughing with delight, her normally sedate friend followed Liz's lead in tempting partners onto the dance floor. Two casual acquaintances were only too happy to oblige. The music swelled. The champagne flowed. Liz laughed. The lights grew brighter. The scent of flowers and expensive perfume grew stronger. One smiling face seemed to melt into the next.

At six the next morning, while Liz held an ice pack to her throbbing head, she admitted what had become obvious as last evening had advanced. She would have enjoyed herself more with Aunt Eugenia and the smug but undoubtedly attractive Nathan Hollister. And she wouldn't have such a splitting headache now.

If only Jim had been more attentive, Liz thought. Maybe then she wouldn't have indulged in so much champagne. But Jim had ignored her most of the night. Even when Liz dragged him onto the dance floor he had been stiff and unresponsive. Liz had been sick of him well before he drove her and Maggie home. As a candidate, she would still back him a hundred percent. As a man, she was going to file him in the "case closed" section of her little black book.

"If I had a little black book." Admitting, even to herself, how empty her social calendar was brought a groan to Liz's lips.

"What's wrong?" Maggie whispered from the doorway of Liz's guest bedroom.

"I think I died." Struggling to a sitting position on the couch, Liz watched her friend make her way gingerly across the apartment. "How are you feeling?"

"Like Ricky Ricardo is playing the congas in my head. Why did I drink? I never drink."

Liz lay back down on the couch. "Did we make fools of ourselves last night?"

"I think so," Maggie muttered. "The last thing I really remember was refusing to let Paul take me home."

"That's how you wound up here."

"If Cassandra was here, it'd be just like old times."

Thinking of their flamboyant friend, Liz attempted a smile that quickly dissolved into a grimace. "Then three of us would have hangovers. Cassandra *always* drank too much champagne. You and I were the sensible ones."

Maggie eased herself down in the overstuffed chair opposite Liz. She closed her eyes. "Remember what Aunt Eugenia always told us about champagne?"

"No more than a glass an hour will keep you from feeling sour," Liz recited.

"Why didn't we listen to her?"

Liz had no answer. Not listening to her aunt about champagne was like not listening to her about men who could take your breath away. It was foolish. With that thought, Nathan Hollister's face rose, clear as any photograph, in Liz's mind.

"Damn Aunt Eugenia for always being right," Liz muttered, wincing as the sound of her own voice pierced her temples.

Weak morning sunshine spilled through the window and across Eugenia's desk. She glanced up from the letter she was writing and looked outside, noting the leafless trees and browning grass. December. Another year almost gone.

Her sigh was not unhappy. Having lived her life exactly as she pleased, Eugenia was packing no regrets to carry through the rest of her days. And she was too busy to worry much about getting older. She still had her health. She had her charities, her family and friends, and if she found herself with an idle moment, she had a wealth of memories to keep her company. Her life was as fulfilling now as it had ever been.

Maybe more so, she decided, putting down her pen and settling back in her chair.

Eugenia knew most people would be surprised to know she counted the last twenty years as the very best of her life. After all, she had lived on three continents. She had made good on her youthful pledge to see and do it all—whatever "it" might be. But when she had traveled enough, when she had grown weary of strange sights and sounds, she had come home to what was most familiar. An old house on a quiet street. Maple trees flaming red in the autumn. Honey bees buzzing in the summer. Eugenia's niece and her husband—Liz's parents—had welcomed her into their household, had allowed her to share their daughter. Liz and her friends had filled Eugenia's life with love. For that she was profoundly grateful.

Liz and Maggie and Cassandra. The children Eugenia had never found time to have. The joy of her heart. Her fond gaze fell on a framed snapshot of the girls. Arms linked, they had posed for this photograph nearly twelve years ago, during Liz's high school graduation party. Eugenia could remember that night as if it were yesterday. That night she had given them her favorite pieces of jewelry. A pearl necklace for gentle Maggie. A ruby ring for fiery Cassandra. And to Liz, as solid as she was brilliant, Eugenia gave her most treasured diamond earrings.

The gifts had been valuable, but to Eugenia the gesture had been purely symbolic. She wanted each of "her" girls to never forget their individuality, to remember they had something unique and infinitely precious to offer the world.

Once more Eugenia's gaze settled on the photograph. How proud she had been of the girls that night. She was still proud. Liz was a successful attorney. Maggie had survived that foolish young marriage and now ran her own decorating firm. And Cassandra? Well, she wasn't exactly turning the New York stage on its ear, but she was busy and happy. The only thing that disappointed Eugenia was that all three of her girls were entering their thirties—alone.

It wasn't that Eugenia gave credence to any claptrap about a woman being incomplete without a man. Yet she couldn't help but believe that life was richer, fuller and more invigorating when shared. Though she had never married, she had known the warmth of sharing. And those memories insulated her from the cold bite of loneliness. She wanted those sorts of memories for her girls. Especially for Liz.

Her niece was so much like her. When Liz believed in something, she dug in her heels and refused to budge. She was intelligent, beautiful, warm and loving. But all those attributes were meant to be shared.

Eugenia was going to make sure they were. She'd only been waiting until she found the right man.

Opening the center desk drawer, she dug through a pile of papers until she located a small leather pouch. The ribbon tied around it was faded and brittle, as were the letters she emptied onto the desk. The scent of per-

fume mingled with the dust that rose in a shaft of sun-
light.

Eugenia took a deep breath as the memories flooded
back. Chanel. Moonlit nights. A breathtaking man by
your side. Yes, her niece deserved that kind of romance.

The kind only a man such as Nathan Hollister could
provide.

Two

Nashville looked good to Nathan on this early December afternoon. This morning he had rented an office suite and hired a secretary. Over lunch, he had tested the business waters with one of the men he had met at last night's party. This afternoon he was going to have tea with Eugenia. He thought tea would have more impact on his life than either of the other two events.

Getting to know a person of Eugenia's position in the community was just good business. She could introduce Nathan to the sort of people he needed to know. But he also liked her. That had been a pleasant surprise. From his father Nathan had learned that success depended not only on what you knew but who you knew. However, he had discovered that the people he needed to know weren't always the ones he would have chosen as friends. That wasn't the case with Eugenia.

Just thinking of the energetic, cosmopolitan woman brought a smile to his lips as he swung his car into the entrance of a curving driveway.

Eugenia's home was huge—three stories of mellowed brick and stone. Ivy climbed to the eaves. A fence framed the lawn, and ancient trees towered above. The setting reminded Nathan of Memphis and the house where his grandfather still ruled amid decaying elegance.

No decay evident here, he observed, approaching the front door. Like polished silver, the windows reflected the late afternoon sun. The immaculate lawn was free of early winter debris. Even the brass door knocker was buffed to high perfection. Unlike his grandfather's house, this home was a testament to the continuing power of old money.

Eugenia answered the door herself. "Do come in," she said, and her blue eyes crinkled at the corners as she smiled. "I was watching for you."

Nathan took her arm as they crossed the entry foyer, chatting. Eugenia was without a doubt one of the easiest people to talk with that he'd ever met. After they left last night's party, she had entertained him with stories of her adventures in Europe. She was plain-spoken and unpretentious, quite different from what one would expect of a person with her kind of money.

"I called Grandfather today to tell him I'd met you," Nathan said. "He wasn't surprised to hear you're still beautiful."

Eugenia patted his hand. "You do wonders for a woman's ego."

The room they entered was brightened by bold splashes of color in the paintings and furniture upholstery. Eugenia's emerald dress blended perfectly. It was the exact color her niece had worn to the party, Nathan decided.

Eugenia had talked a lot about Liz last night. Her college and law school career. Her work in the public defender's office. Her romantically unattached state. *Last night had been lucky, indeed,* Nathan, mused, remembering Liz's brilliant blue eyes and the kissable slant of her red lips. Smiling, he looked around the room again.

"You obviously decorated this room," he said, his gaze skimming from the very French silk-paneled screen in the corner to the African-influenced ivory carvings on the mantel. The blending of styles was uniquely pleasing—like Eugenia herself.

"Liz's mother calls this room my hodgepodge. The rest of the house has benefitted from her exquisite taste, of course."

"I like it."

Chuckling, Eugenia patted the sofa cushion beside her. "Come sit down, you flatterer. We'll have tea as soon as my other guest arrives."

"Who is—"

"You must tell me more of what brings you to Nashville," Eugenia cut in, ignoring his question. "All we talked about last night was me and my family."

Nathan recognized a dodge when he heard it. He acquiesced gracefully, though. He had a feeling he already knew Eugenia's other guest.

"Never again will I drink so much champagne," Liz vowed as she pulled her car to a halt. At least not on a weeknight, she added silently.

She winced as her brakes squealed and frowned as she glanced at her watch. She was late. Again. She had been running behind schedule all day, and that hadn't gone over too well with her office full of clients. She should be back at the office now, going over last-minute details for the Bartlett case, but she hated disappointing Aunt Eugenia. Their Thursday afternoon tea had become a tradition, and Liz continued to make time for it whenever she could.

She slammed her car door and studied the unfamiliar red Corvette parked in the driveway of her parents' home. The classic car's high-gloss paint only emphasized the dusty condition of her own five-year-old Datsun. But Liz patted her car's hood affectionately. "Baby, when I get the time I promise you a bath."

As usual she disregarded the front entrance and hurried down a flagstone path to a side door. The kitchen was filled with the delicious smell of homemade cookies, and a plump, gray-haired woman turned to greet her. "Ah, Liz, I knew that would be you."

Liz dropped a kiss on the woman's smooth cheek. "ESP, Jeannette?"

"No, the sound of your brakes." Two decades in America had not destroyed Jeannette's French accent, and never was it more pronounced than when she was about to scold someone. Liz knew this reproachful tone well.

She protested, "Jeannette, you couldn't possibly have heard my brakes here in the kitchen."

"Ah, but I heard them last week, and I know my Liz, and therefore I know they are still squeaking. You take care of everyone but yourself."

"Just because you were an ambulance driver in the war does not mean you're an expert on cars."

"*Chérie*, it takes no expert to know when brakes are going bad," the woman retorted, her loose topknot of hair shaking as she tossed her head. "You will make me crazy someday."

"You've been saying that ever since you arrived with Aunt Eugenia, and Maggie and Cassandra and I hid your suitcases. Surely by now you should have been in an insane asylum."

Jeannette's brown eyes sparkled. "Before that I will go back to Paris where a little craziness is appreciated."

Merely grinning in reply, Liz reached across the cart for a cookie.

"Stop that," Jeannette instructed sternly, sounding just as she had when Liz was twelve. "Tea will be served in the front parlor."

"I'll take it in." Pushing the cart toward the hall, Liz tossed a question over her shoulder. "Who's the guest in the fancy car?"

"A friend of your aunt's," Jeannette returned blandly. A trifle too blandly, Liz thought.

Suspicious, she pressed, "Anyone I know?"

The Frenchwoman threw up her hands. "And how should I know that, *chérie*? I am not the keeper of the guestbook."

"I was just asking."

"Just leave me to my kitchen—and make sure you don't eat all those cookies."

"Yes, please don't eat all the cookies."

The deep male voice brought Liz's head spinning around in surprise, and she found herself staring into Nathan Hollister's amused hazel eyes. *I should have known when I saw that obscenely slick car. It suits him so well.*

Before Liz could speak, Aunt Eugenia was bustling through the doorway behind Nathan. She looked very small beside his solid masculine frame. "I see you've hijacked the tea cart, Liz."

"I was just bringing it in."

Eugenia pretended to ignore her niece's baleful glance. "Nathan and I were beginning to wonder if you or the tea were ever going to arrive. You do remember Nathan, don't you?" she asked, all innocence.

I was hoping to forget him, Liz wanted to say. Instead she schooled her voice and her expression into polite indifference. "From last night? Of course. Hello, Mr. Hollister."

He took the hand she offered. And held on to it. An annoying habit of his, Liz decided, though she could feel her indifference slip as his strong fingers gave hers a slight squeeze. In gray tweed jacket and black slacks, he was every bit as impressive as he'd been last night in a tuxedo. And he knew it, too, judging from the smug expression on his handsome face.

"I was hoping I'd see you again." His husky voice managed to give the words more than casual significance.

Liz caught the pleased glance that passed between Eugenia and Jeannette. *Busybodies.* No doubt they were expecting quite a show—with Liz resisting the expertly choreographed advances of this oh-so-charming man. Well, they were going to be disappointed. She would be as sweet as honey to him.

Accordingly she slanted him a coquettish glance. "Mr. Hollister, I must say I've been thinking about you, too." That much wasn't untrue. His face had intruded on her thoughts at the oddest moments ever since this morning.

"Have you?" His fingers tightened on hers.

"Yes," Liz murmured, and this time the breathless note in her voice was no pretense. A dangerous development. "Shouldn't we be having tea?" She extricated her hand from his but continued to smile up at him for Eugenia and Jeannette's benefit. Pushing the tea cart toward the hall, Liz glanced at her aunt. "Coming?"

Eugenia regarded her strangely agreeable niece with wariness, but she said nothing as she led the way to the front parlor.

Perched on the couch beside Eugenia, Liz poured their tea from a gleaming silver pot while Nathan settled in a wing chair.

He took his cup and chose several cookies. "This reminds me of the teas my grandmother used to have."

"Your grandmother was a lovely girl." Eugenia leaned back, her smile dreamy with remembrance. "Mind you, I never quite forgave her for stealing your grandfather from me, but I liked her just the same."

Nathan laughed. "Something tells me the only men ever stolen from you were those you didn't really want."

While her aunt beamed, Liz arched an eyebrow at his smoothness. "Tell me, Aunt Eugenia. Was your Mr. Hollister as quick with the compliments as his grandson?"

"Oh, my, he was worse."

"Hard to believe," Liz murmured dryly, momentarily forgetting her vow to be charming. Her gaze locked with Nathan's as she took a sip of tea.

She's sharp, Nathan decided, tipping his cup to her in a silent salute. He usually avoided women this sharp, no matter how beautiful they were. But he didn't want to avoid Liz. And at this particular moment, as he studied her lovely, flushed face, his reasons for wanting to know her better had little to do with her family's connections. That realization unsettled him. Much as he liked Eugenia, as intriguing as he found Liz, it was what they could do for him and his business that was most important. Wasn't it?

Trying to shake off that hint of doubt, Nathan asked her, "I am going to have the pleasure of meeting your parents, aren't I?"

"They're in Europe. Daddy retired last year—"

"He was a judge, right?"

"Yes." Liz's eyes softened with affection. "He and Mother have always wanted to spend a year abroad. They're not planning to come home till spring."

Eugenia interrupted before Nathan could reply. "Liz, Nathan has moved his firm and himself to Nashville."

"I'm not really moving a business," Nathan corrected Eugenia, looking at Liz. "I've left the public relations firm I was with in Memphis, and I'm opening my own here in Nashville. I've retained some clients who are based here."

"Well, whatever," Eugenia said airily. "I think it's marvelous. Don't you, Liz?"

Not answering, she gulped down some hot tea.

Amused, Nathan set his own cup down on the end table. "I think your niece's opinion of my work is well documented, Eugenia. Let's not put her on the spot."

"Liz is just miffed because her candidate lost that silly election. She hates to lose."

"Then we have something in common," Nathan murmured.

Trying to appear unconcerned, Liz reached for a sandwich. "First of all, the election wasn't silly, and second, I'm no longer miffed, Aunt Eugenia. I think it's perfectly wonderful that Nathan is opening a firm here." *Just what the city needs,* she added to herself, *another sleazebag publicity mill.*

Eugenia chuckled in delight. "I'm so glad you feel that way, Liz. Because I want you and Nathan to work together."

The bread and cream cheese lodged in Liz's throat, but she resisted the urge to cough when she caught Nathan's knowing glance. She swallowed hard. "I really don't know that our office has any need—"

Eugenia interrupted, "I'm referring to the auction."

"Auction?" Nathan asked.

"Aunt Eugenia's favorite charity project is a camp for underprivileged children," Liz explained. "Every year she puts together an auction to raise money."

Eugenia nodded. "I certainly don't do it on my own. Lots of others are involved—everyone from country-music people to businessmen. You'd enjoy helping, Nathan."

And benefit from it, too, Nathan thought. In the course of working on the auction, he'd be rubbing elbows with the people he most wanted to know. The heads of successful companies. Politicians. Men and women with power to wield. The campaign he had won for Hugo Mantooth was a good beginning for his firm, but to grow quickly he could use automatic acceptance from the people who mattered in this town.

Besides, it would give him the chance to get to know Liz Patterson. His glance slid down the length of slender leg her camel-colored skirt revealed. Yes, knowing Liz could be very interesting. "I'd love to help," he agreed.

"Good!" Eugenia turned to her niece. "I can count on you, can't I?"

Liz had been involved with the auction since Eugenia had started it twelve years ago, and during summer breaks from college she had worked as a counselor at the camp. She very much wanted to stay in touch with what had become a family project. But not with Nathan Hollister in tow.

"You know I'll help," she told her aunt. "However—"

Eugenia didn't allow Liz to register any protest. "Then it's settled—you and Nathan will handle all the publicity this year."

"But I did it all last year," Liz said. "It's really just a one-person job, and if Nathan wants—"

"I know I'll need your help," he insisted.

"But publicity is your business."

"But you already know all about the auction."

"And this has to be the most successful auction ever," Eugenia added, heaving a dramatic sigh. "It may be my last."

Liz glared at her. Eugenia's tragic look was pure invention. She was healthier than many people half her age. "You know you'll be running this auction well into the twenty-first century."

Somehow Eugenia managed to look pitiful. She placed a hand over her heart. "One never knows, Liz."

The theatrics of the moment weren't lost on Nathan, but he suppressed a smile and played along. "Liz, I promise to be cooperative. We don't want to upset Eugenia."

Eugenia sighed again. "Yes, it would be nice for everything to go smoothly this year."

"All right, all right," Liz agreed with ill-concealed impatience. It really wasn't worth any hassles. A few hours spent in Nathan Hollister's company might not be completely impossible. "I guess we'll be working together."

"Wonderful!" Miraculously retreating from death's door, Eugenia rose from the couch. "Why don't you two start making plans? If you'll excuse me, I just remembered something I have to tell Jeannette."

Very convenient, Liz thought, watching her aunt leave.

"Does Eugenia always get what she wants?" Nathan asked.

"Just about."

Her terse reply amused him. "I'm sorry you don't like me, Liz."

"It isn't that—"

"I must have done something to annoy you. A few minutes ago you said you'd been thinking about me."

Guiltily, Liz realized he was right. She should never have acted so flirtatious. She would correct that right now. "I never said my thoughts of you had been pleasant."

His laughter was deep and rich. "You inherited more than your looks from Eugenia."

Feeling cocky, she tossed her head. "Yes, I usually get what I want, too."

Nathan's expression sobered, but a twinkle remained in his hazel eyes. "I'll keep that in mind."

"Actually, I think working with me on this will be good for you," Liz added primly.

"Really?"

"Publicizing this kind of event will call for more *above-board* tactics than you usually employ."

"I thought you weren't still miffed about that election."

Now Liz smiled. "I'm not."

"I didn't start those rumors."

"I know." She didn't know why, but she believed him. "But that still doesn't change my opinion of some of your other tactics."

"Because you have a personal interest in Jim Levinson?" Though Eugenia had indicated otherwise, Nathan thought Liz might be involved with the former candidate. That didn't matter, but he liked to know what he was up against.

"Jim is a friend, nothing more."

"Then perhaps you'll have dinner with me tonight."

He doesn't waste much time, Liz thought. "I think not."

"Don't we need to discuss the auction?"

"The auction isn't until March. It can wait until after Christmas."

"Then can't you just take pity on a stranger in town?" Nathan appealed, adopting his best lonely bachelor look.

Liz couldn't help but laugh. "You were acting quite at home at that party last night."

"That was business. I'll be all alone tonight." His hazel eyes were wide, his expression deceptively innocent.

To her surprise, Liz found herself thinking about giving in to him. But true to form, she resisted. "I don't even know you."

"I'll tell you anything you want to know." Nathan leaned forward, the very picture of earnest entreaty. "I'm thirty-five. Single. Never married. My parents divorced when I was five. My father and I lived with my grandparents. Dad was in banking—"

"How about references?" Liz cut in, laughing again.

"Eugenia knows my family. Isn't that good enough?"

"She's not always as picky as I am."

Looking comically discouraged, Nathan ran a hand through his already-tumbled hair. The gesture made him curiously appealing. Too appealing. Liz had to remind herself that he wasn't her type at all. No matter what Eugenia's opinion was. No matter that Liz had thought about him all day. No, he was one headache she should steer clear of. "I'm sorry, but I really can't go anywhere tonight. I'm due in court tomorrow, and I've got work to do."

"Important case?"

"I consider them all important."

"Somehow I knew you'd say that," Nathan said, grinning. "But since this case is keeping you from having dinner with me, it must be a big one."

Egotist, Liz thought, even as she explained. "As a matter of fact, there's this kid—"

"Thief, rapist or murderer?"

"You sound just like Aunt Eugenia."

Nathan's expression sobered. "She worries about you."

"Too much," Liz added. "For a woman who took off for Europe when she was barely of age, she's become awfully protective of me."

"I think that's a common affliction in people her age. My grandfather was a notorious scoundrel in his day, and now he's after me to settle down."

"It gets annoying, doesn't it?"

"Oh, I don't know." Again, Nathan rubbed a hand through his hair, and the gold band of his watch flashed. "Maybe I should listen to him."

Sending him a skeptical glance, Liz poured them both another cup of tea. "Men who drive cars like yours are not looking to settle down."

He accepted his cup and leaned back again. "Then what am I looking for?"

She answered impulsively. "Someone to go along for the ride." She wasn't referring to his car.

"Interested?"

That single drawled word ranked right at the top of the sexiest invitations Liz had ever received. She paused, teacup halfway to her lips, trying to gauge whether or not he was serious. The boldness of his gaze said he was. For a moment she allowed an answering excitement to skip through her, and she could feel the color rushing to her face. Then she took a deep swallow of tea and forced a light note into her voice. "Very blunt, aren't you?"

"I'm just honest."

"I bet you can be very subtle, too, when it suits you."

"I can be whatever it takes to get what I want." There was a confident, very masculine gleam in his eyes.

"Then you're really not honest at all."

"I'm honest about my dishonesties."

"That's a piece of twisted logic if I ever heard one."

He laughed and shrugged his broad shoulders nonchalantly. "How did logic get into this conversation? In my experience logic has little to do with why people do what they do."

"Perhaps you don't know the right sort of people."

"Are you offering to change that?"

Liz gave him a grudging smile. "You don't give up, do you?"

He shook his head. "I told you I don't like to lose."

"Is this a contest?"

"If you make it one."

"What are we competing for?"

"I'm sorry. I thought I made that very clear." Deliberately, Nathan allowed his gaze to slip from her face and down her body, coming to rest again on her very visible and very attractive crossed legs.

Liz had to fight the urge to tug her skirt down. No witty retort sprang to mind, either. She merely glared at Nathan as he selected another cookie from the tray. His smile was decidedly smug. Smothering an oath, she set her cup and saucer down with a clatter and got up to look out the window.

This man was quite a case, all right. Handsome. Slick as a polished stone. Charming but brash. He was everything she disliked. Yet she found him extremely attractive. That was most unsettling, and it was exactly why Liz was going to keep her distance.

"So, have you changed your mind?"

She turned from the window, surprised by his question. "Changed my mind about what?"

"About dinner tonight."

Thinking him the most self-confident person she had ever met, Liz couldn't help but admire his tenaciousness. But she wasn't going to dinner or anywhere else with him, tonight or any night. "I told you I have to work."

"But isn't that just an excuse?" Nathan had stood, and now he came across the room, stopping close to Liz. Too close. She caught the musky scent of his aftershave and noticed again how long and black and curly his lashes were. Such a contrast to his tawny hair.

"I don't make excuses," she said, annoyed by the shakiness his nearness caused inside her.

The amused glimmer was back in his eyes. "No excuses. No apologies. No explanations. My, my, Liz— you and I are more alike than I thought."

"Only when you twist my words."

Nathan liked the glow that anger gave her skin. She'd looked like this last night when Eugenia had introduced them. "Righteous indignation becomes you," he murmured. Following an impulse, he touched his fingers to her cheek. *Like rose petals,* he had time to think before she jerked away.

"Mr. Hollister," she began in a cold voice.

"So we're back to that, Miss Patterson?"

"Yes, we are." Stiffly, Liz walked across the room, pausing by the doorway to look back at him. "I'll see you sometime after Christmas. If you're still interested in the auction by then, that is."

"I will be," he answered laconically.

"I'm sure that by then you'll have your pick of dinner companions. No doubt the female population of Nashville will have discovered your car, your Rolex and your smooth line—which, by the way, is a little too smooth. I'd work on that if I were you. A few rough edges are always more interesting."

His bow was flippant. "Thanks for the advice."

"No problem."

Liz turned on her heel and left him standing by the window. She was halfway across the shadowy foyer when she realized she was holding her breath. As she paused at the bottom of the stairway, she glimpsed a flash of green disappearing through another doorway.

"Aunt Eugenia," she called in a voice loud enough for Nathan to hear. "If you wanted to know what we were discussing, you should have planted a bug. Eavesdropping is so unladylike."

Masculine laughter sounded from the room she had just left, but Liz didn't bother to wait for a reply from her aunt. She hurried to the kitchen, retrieved her purse and left without speaking to Jeannette, who stood by her stove, a knowing smile on her lips as she stirred a pot of stew.

And it was only when Liz had reached her car that she put a hand to the cheek Nathan Hollister had touched. The hand shook. She dropped her keys. She cursed him. But there was a curiously buoyant feeling inside her, a tiny ballooning of feminine satisfaction. It was always nice to be desired, even pursued.

From the window, Nathan watched her leave and smiled once again. For a man who had been turned down—twice—he was feeling oddly triumphant. But then, he had always enjoyed a challenge, especially when the prize was a beautiful woman. This time the beauty came with brains. This could be a very interesting pursuit.

"Well, Nathan," Eugenia said as she joined him by the window. "I guess you're onto my game, aren't you?"

"Your game?" He cocked an eyebrow. "I thought I was calling the shots."

She chuckled heartily. "I think we're interested in different stakes, my boy."

"Maybe not." Avoiding Eugenia's sharp gaze, he looked out the window again. "You just leave Plan B up to me."

Unlike the crowded courtrooms of television dramas, the room Nathan slipped into was half empty. He took a seat midway to the front, the perfect vantage point from which to study Liz.

She looked every inch a professional, her slim shoulders straight, her chestnut hair coiled in a neat bun at the nape of her neck. With two other lawyers she approached the judge, and when she returned to her seat, Nathan saw the jaunty red handkerchief tucked into the pocket of her gray suit. He nodded in approval. Red meant confidence.

Evidently the trial was nearing its end. While one of the other lawyers rose to present his closing remarks, Nathan relaxed and watched Liz.

For almost a week he had been trying to see her. Lunch and dinner invitations had been left via messages to her office and her home answering machine. Polite refusals had been extended by the efficient voice of Liz's secretary. No excuses were given. Just "no thanks." Nathan respected the honesty, but he wasn't accustomed to being refused. He definitely wasn't giving up. Yesterday he had sent flowers and a note.

Why was he so fascinated? It was more than Liz's social connections. He could use whatever rewards being her escort might bring, but not even that could keep Nathan Hollister in the game when the interest wasn't reciprocated. It was also more than the challenge she presented. He had other challenges on his mind right now—such as getting his business successfully off the ground. No, he had not one logical reason for his unrelenting pursuit of Liz Patterson. Because logic had nothing to do with the petal softness of her skin.

Nathan clenched his hand into a fist, remembering the smoothness of her cheek under his fingers as they had stood in Eugenia's front parlor. He could see the angry flash of her blue eyes, hear the faintly amused sound of her voice.

Abruptly his attention snapped back to the courtroom. He *was* hearing Liz's voice. While his thoughts drifted, she had taken the floor and was in front of the jury, presenting her closing argument. She would have them believe her client had played no role in a convenience store holdup last summer. The woman had been duped by her boyfriend. She didn't know he had a gun. She didn't know he had planned the robbery. She had driven him away from the store because he had threatened the lives of her children if she didn't.

Nathan leaned forward, letting Liz's arguments wind around him. Her words were carefully chosen. Every gesture was used to articulate a point. He believed her. More importantly, she had the jury eating out of her hand. Damn but she's good, he thought, wondering at his surprise.

The adrenaline was pumping through Liz. It was always this way when she believed in her client. She felt invincible. Turning away from the jury, she paused, ready to give her speech its final punch. Then she saw Nathan. And her concentration broke. For a moment she stared at him. He grinned. She stumbled over her words and spun away from his scrutiny, gathering her composure to continue the summation. The slipup was minuscule. But Liz was fuming inside, furious with herself for letting his presence rattle her. Nothing—no one—had rattled her since the early days of her career.

He was waiting for her in the corridor after court was adjourned. Leaning against the wall in his tweed jacket and navy slacks, he looked very handsome, a little bored and as always, faintly amused. Liz was tempted to just walk right by him. As could be expected, he didn't give her a chance.

"Counselor, that was a brilliant performance," he drawled, falling in step beside her.

"Thank you."

Nathan smiled at her grim expression. "What's wrong? Don't you think you're going to win?"

Ignoring the question, Liz stopped in the middle of the corridor. "What brings you to these hallowed halls of justice anyway, Mr. Hollister? Just in the neighborhood?"

"I got curious about the case that's been keeping us apart."

Liz laughed dryly. "Nothing is keeping us apart but me."

"Really?"

"I believe my secretary—"

"—is getting tired of my calls. You could have at least talked to me yourself."

"I'm the one who's getting tired of you," Liz snapped, her voice louder than she'd intended. The heads of several passing colleagues swiveled her way. Biting back a curse, she stalked to the side of the corridor, confident Nathan would follow. He did, but he didn't give her time to protest further.

"Did you get my flowers?"

"Yes, and—"

"My note?" he pressed.

A hot flush crawled up Liz's neck. Attached to the three ivory roses had been a card which said simply, "They reminded me of your skin." No name had been enclosed, but Liz had known the handwriting was Nathan's.

Any sensible woman would have thrown the flowers and the message in the trash. But even now the card was in her purse. The roses were in a vase on her desk. Just this morning she had touched the petals and thought about him. She was enjoying his attention. Knowing that, her gaze skittered nervously away from his.

"Don't you like roses?" he asked, bracing one arm against the wall as he leaned closer.

Through her jacket, Liz could feel the cool marble of the wall against her back. She didn't like being cornered. Her chin lifted as she looked up at him. "Of course I like them, but—"

"No buts, please."

"But I still don't—"

"Sh." Nathan silenced her by placing his fingers gently against her mouth. To his surprise, there was nothing gentle about the desire that ripped through him.

Strangely unable to move, Liz watched raw emotion replace the usual cool expression on Nathan's face. She had wondered if that facade ever slipped. She had her answer now, but the knowledge was oddly disturbing. Their gazes remained locked as his fingers fell away from her lips. One finger lightly traced her jawline and feathered down to her slender neck. Liz caught her breath. He leaned closer.

"Let's get out of here," he whispered.

Slowly she shook her head, not trusting her voice.

"Please."

"I can't," she managed.

"Why?"

"Work."

A skeptical gleam crept into his hazel eyes. "You're making excuses."

"No, I'm not."

"What about dinner?"

Liz started to say yes. Then she caught herself. Nathan Hollister had her exactly where he wanted her.

Pressed to the wall, patently ready for seduction. She had never been such an easy target for any man's charm, and she wasn't giving in so fast. This one he would really have to work for.

With her free hand, she touched the knot in his silk tie and smiled at him. "I'm afraid the answer is still no, Nathan."

For a moment his face registered surprised. Then he straightened away from her, his cool mask back in place.

"I just don't want to go out with you," she added.

"You will." He pressed something soft in her palm, his strong hand closing her fingers around it. Then he was gone, not looking back as his easy, rolling stride carried him away from her.

Liz gazed after him, not feeling the triumph she had anticipated. When he was out of sight, she opened her hand. She held a fist full of rose petals, their tips brown and crushed. Their flowershop aroma drifted upward, and Liz let them flutter to the floor. Were they meant as a threat? Or a promise?

Squaring her shoulders, she started walking. A smile touched her lips as she wondered what Nathan's next move would be.

From a phone booth in the lobby, Nathan watched Liz leave the building, noting her smile. So she was wavering. Good. Damn, but he was beginning to really enjoy himself. He punched in a number and waited for an answer.

"Hello?"

"I think it's time for Plan C," he said, not bothering to identify himself.

Eugenia chuckled. "Not as easy as you thought, huh?"

"She's almost ready to crack."

"No prizes for almost, my boy," she replied, her firm voice reminding Nathan of his father. Second place had never counted with him, either.

"You're right," Nathan murmured. "What's your plan?"

Three

Spurred by an icy wind, Liz hurried into the house. The
entry foyer was warm and smelled of the pine needles in
a holiday arrangement on the table by the door. Miniature lights twinkled in the garland on the stairway's
curving banister. Soft music and laughter floated from
a room down the hall. As usual for the holidays, Aunt
Eugenia had infused the house with festive cheer.

"You're late again, *chérie*."

Liz smiled at Jeannette, who was hurrying from the
back of the house, looking crisp and neat in her black
uniform.

"I'm always late," Liz said, shrugging out of her
velvet evening cape.

Her brown eyes shrewd, Jeannette took the wrap.
"You work too hard."

The admonishment was familiar and perhaps true,
but Liz ignored it as she turned to adjust her earrings in

the mirror beside the door. Her face was too pale against the brilliant diamonds and her vivid red taffeta dress. The dress had probably been a poor choice, but there hadn't been time to dawdle over wardrobe selection tonight. After a surprising two days of deliberation, the jury had returned their verdict at five. Liz had lost.

Her shoulders drooped a little as she remembered. She had been so sure she would win. Perhaps too sure. Now her client, who was only nineteen, faced several years in prison and separation from her children. No matter what the jury had decided, Liz just couldn't believe the young woman had been a willing accomplice in the robbery. She was just another victim, fallen prey to the charm of a man, and Liz had failed her. What could she have done differently?

A light touch on Liz's arm brought her back to the present. She looked up and found Jeannette regarding her with concern.

"Everyone is in the middle parlor," the housekeeper said. "You should join them. Go have some fun. You look as if you need it."

Patting Jeannette's hand, Liz silently agreed with her. If Aunt Eugenia hadn't decided to throw this dinner party for the auction committee, Liz probably would have spent the evening alone in her apartment, brooding. This was much better, even if she was certain to see Nathan Hollister. Or maybe *because* she would see him. Turning away from that line of thought, Liz went down the hall.

She saw him immediately. At the center of a group of earnest-looking men, he was easily the tallest person present. His hair was less unruly than usual. His dark suit was very correct. Their eyes met, and she expected him to join her. Instead he returned to his conversation, and Liz knew a moment's disappointment, followed quickly by irritation. Her chin tilted upward. She didn't care if he paid any attention to her.

Eugenia called a greeting from her seat at the room's center. With the exception of Nathan, the acknowledgment was echoed by most of the twenty-odd guests, and Liz was soon circulating with wineglass in hand. As usual, Eugenia had assembled an interesting group for the auction committee. Nashville's old guard mingled comfortably with the inevitable politicians and the reigning king and queen of country music. Conversation ranged from fashion to the stock market to the auction. Liz found her friend Maggie in a corner, discussing a decorating job with a client.

"No shop talk," she scolded them playfully. "This is supposed to be a party."

Maggie's companion laughed and took herself off to have her drink freshened.

"Only the third drink she's had in half an hour," Maggie whispered to Liz.

"You shouldn't talk about paying customers."

Giving a rueful chuckle, Maggie shook her head. "Who said she pays? All she wants is free advice. She was one of Mother's friends."

Liz nodded in sympathy.

"He's interesting, isn't he?" Maggie murmured.

"Who?" Liz asked, though she could guess to whom Maggie referred.

"Him, of course." Maggie nodded toward Nathan. He was now sitting beside Eugenia, laughing at whatever she was saying. His laughter was as rich and smooth as warm honey.

Liz cleared her throat and pretended indifference. "He's okay, I guess."

"He's been watching you ever since you got here."

"Don't be silly," Liz protested. "He hasn't even spoken to me." Though she tried to contain it, a bit of feminine pique crept into her voice.

That obviously didn't escape Maggie's notice. Her brown eyes were teasing. "I'm going to talk to him next week about decorating his office."

"How nice."

"Don't you want to know more?"

"No." Liz drained the last of her wine. "Goodness, I think I need another drink myself. Excuse me." She left Maggie and crossed to the bar.

Liz noticed that Nathan immediately went to the opposite side of the room. Their gazes met again, but his slid away once more. She joined the group he was in, and he excused himself. Over the shoulder of an exceedingly boring bank executive, Liz spied him in deep conversation with Maggie. When she could finally move in that direction, he was nowhere to be found until his laughter rang out, again from the other part of the room.

All right, Liz thought grimly, avoid me, Mr. Hollister. Seizing upon the nearest man, she began an animated discussion of the upcoming collegiate bowl games. But hard as she tried, she couldn't stop looking for Nathan. Like participants in an elaborate folk dance, they continued to circle the room and each other.

The dance ended at dinner. At the smaller of two dining tables, Nathan's place card was next to Liz's. Thanks, Eugenia, he thought. Her plan was proceeding just as they had discussed. From the head of the other table, she sent him an encouraging smile.

Liz smiled, too, a trifle too brightly. "Why, Nathan, I haven't even had a chance to say hello."

He held out her chair. "Yes, I've been trying to get to your side all evening."

"Oh, have you?" As she sat, she glanced up at him. He winked, and Liz's smile dimmed a watt or two.

"So how are you?" she said, unfolding her napkin with what Nathan thought was unusual force.

"Very well, and you?" He took his own seat. "Did you win your case?"

The smile disappeared, and Liz's gaze lowered. "No." Before Nathan could react, the gentleman to her right claimed her attention.

Dinner conversation caught Nathan, too, but he found his gaze coming back again and again to Liz. Her features seemed more delicately etched than he remembered, and even her artful makeup couldn't disguise the faint violet shadows under her eyes. She looked tired. Because of the case? He frowned. That had to be a disappointment. If she had conducted the entire trial as brilliantly as she'd managed the closing statement, he couldn't see why she had lost.

He wanted to ask her what had happened, but the opening never came. After dinner she disappeared with Maggie, and for Nathan the party lost its spark. Over coffee in the parlor, he tried to concentrate on being charming. The room was full of valuable contacts. He was surprised to realize he didn't care. He would rather be talking to Liz about her case, about anything. Of course, he assured himself, talking to Liz was business, too. She was just another contact. Wasn't she? Again there was that doubt. Business seemed unimportant next to finding out why she had looked so sad during dinner. When Maggie returned without Liz, he hesitated only a moment before slipping out to look for her.

She was in the room where they'd had tea. A Christmas tree stood in front of the window, and the colorful lights brightened the otherwise dim room. Standing beside the tree, Liz's posture was weary, her expression pensive. Nathan paused in the doorway and decided she needed some cheering up.

"Are you making a Christmas wish?" he said, leaning against the doorjamb.

Liz glanced up. She wasn't at all surprised to see him. Maybe secretly she had been hoping he would find her. Sparring with him would keep her mind off the trial. She smiled. "As a matter of fact I *was* making a wish."

He ambled toward her. She was growing used to his deceptively lazy way of moving. Something told her he could react quickly if the situation asked for it.

"What were you wishing for?" Nathan asked, reaching out to touch one of Eugenia's favorite mirrored tree ornaments. The ball reflected the Christmas lights as it spun round and round, washing colors over Liz's face, bouncing off her dangling, diamond earrings. Her smile faded as quickly as the colors changed.

"Wishes don't come true if you share them."

"And wishes don't change the minds of jurors."

Now he had surprised her. Liz glanced at him, wondering how he could have known she was wishing for another chance for her client.

"You were terrific at the end," he continued. "What went wrong?"

"Who knows?" She shrugged and looked away.

Nathan studied her bowed head. "You don't want to talk about it, do you?"

"No."

"I understand. Every time an account slips through my fingers I don't want to discuss it with anyone for days. That's what I like about having my own firm. I don't have to rehash everything with a boss."

Liz lifted an eyebrow. "Pardon me, but I would hardly compare the loss of an account to my client's jail sentence."

He raised his hands as if to deflect a blow. "Hey, my occupation may be different from yours, but I am allowed to care about it, aren't I?"

He was right. Liz gave him a smile of apology. "I'm sorry. I sometimes get a little intense about my work."

Intense about everything, Nathan corrected silently. "Ever think about leaving the public defender's office?" he asked, fascinated by the play of light across her face.

The shake of her head was emphatic. "I like helping people in need."

"Millionaires need legal advice, too, you know."

"It's not the same."

"No, it pays better."

She sighed in exasperation. "I didn't become a lawyer to make a lot of money."

"Of course not," Nathan retorted, gesturing to their well-appointed surroundings. "You don't need money."

"No, but I'm also a born crusader."

"A champion of underdogs?" he asked, amused.

Liz tossed her head. "Laugh if you want to, but I've always been this way. When I was nine, I organized a school-wide protest against the cafeteria's mystery meat. My father said I argued the case brilliantly, and I won, too."

"I bet you did." Without conscious effort, Nathan caught one of her hands in his. "You're not what someone would expect."

"What do you mean?" Liz liked the feel of her fingers clasped in his. She ignored the warning bell sounding in her head.

"You're not the typical rich bitch."

His frankness brought a delighted giggle to her lips. "What is typical?"

"You know—a Jag in the drive, two husbands by the thirtieth birthday, afternoons at the club."

"How do you know I don't secretly yearn for all those things?"

His expression sobered. "Because a person like that wouldn't be standing by the Christmas tree making a wish for someone else."

Again Liz looked away, and she pulled her hand from his grasp, too. She liked it better when they were arguing. "What about you?" she asked lightly as she rearranged an errant piece of tree garland. "From your family background I would have thought you'd be running for office instead of running other people's campaigns."

"Just lucky, I guess."

"Oh, come on. Why aren't you in Memphis, safely married to your childhood sweetheart, raising your two point three children and managing the family business?"

He laughed, but the sound was oddly mirthless. "The only business my family is in is spending money. I leave that up to my grandfather."

It was the second time he had mentioned money, Liz realized, thinking it odd. Not that there was anything wrong with money, but like most people who had grown up with wealth she rarely mentioned it or gave it a great deal of thought. From the little Eugenia had said about Nathan's grandfather, Liz had just assumed she and Nathan had similar backgrounds.

Curious, she pressed on, "What about your father?"

"He's dead." The words were blunt, devoid of emotion.

I'll have to ask Eugenia more about his family, Liz thought, studying his expressionless face. He was clearly not going to share any insights with her tonight. "I'm sorry," she said quietly.

"Don't be." Nathan sent the mirrored ball spinning again and grasped her hand. "Come for a drive with me."

"A drive?"

His grin was almost irresistible. "The party's winding down. Eugenia won't mind."

"But Nathan—"

"Come on."

She wavered, and he took advantage of her hesitation. They had said goodbye to the others, retrieved their coats and were out the door before she could gather another protest. She even forgot her silent vow to never go anywhere with him. I was right about his moving fast, Liz thought as she slid into the passenger seat of his Corvette.

Nathan rummaged in the space behind the seats. "Here," he said, handing Liz a heavy woolen blanket. "Put up your hood and wrap this around your legs."

Liz paused in the act of buckling her seat belt. "You mean this buggy has no heat?"

"Not tonight." Without pause, he rolled the convertible top back.

Liz gasped as the cold December breeze washed over her again. Tipping her head back, she gazed up at the brilliant stars, and her troubles seemed to slip right off her shoulders.

Nathan pressed the accelerator, and the car purred in response. "Are you ready?" he asked, strapping on his seat belt.

Liz lifted her hood and shouted over the roar of the engine. "You're crazy, do you know that?"

"Yep." He pulled his collar up around his neck and grinned. "Hang on."

The car jumped forward, tires squealing, and the wind caught Liz's laughter. She imagined the sound was spinning up into the clear sky like some out-of-control *Star Wars* spacecraft. And she laughed some more.

It was the wildest ride of her life. They roared through the sedate streets of her childhood and streaked onto the interstate. The lights of the city blurred into neon ribbons. Nathan's Fuzz Buster shrieked warning after warning. The frigid wind stung her cheeks. She could taste the cold. It combined with her excitement, and she realized she liked the flavor.

Recklessness had never been Liz's style. In the pranks of her childhood she had been the voice of reason, the one who kept daredevil Cassandra and gullible Maggie out of trouble. Liz had always played by the rules. She stopped at every stop sign and returned any salesclerk's overpayment in change. Other people might eat two double fudge sundaes and then hide their guilt by setting the bathroom scales back. Liz would eat only one sundae and compulsively make up for it by speed walking an extra mile at the track. Only in the courtroom did she take chances.

But maybe she had been playing it too safe, she decided as the car continued to hurtle through the night. Every mile released another tight coil of tension inside her. Her senses were spinning. Maybe there was something to be said for losing control every once in a while. She suspected Nathan often followed his impulses, and judging by his shouts of pleasure as he dodged in and out of traffic, he enjoyed himself tremendously. It might do her good to walk on the wild side, too. Nathan was the perfect companion for the journey. Undoubtedly he broke more rules than he obeyed.

She was windblown, frozen, but still laughing when the car screeched to a halt at the Opryland Hotel. The parking lot was full of people entering and exiting the popular attraction, and it seemed to Liz they all stopped to stare at her and Nathan.

"I guess people around here don't see many convertibles," he commented as he helped Liz out of the car.

"Not with the tops down in twenty-degree weather."

"How odd."

Liz laughed again, though she did hope no one she knew was around. Her friends and colleagues would think she'd had too much champagne, just like at last week's party. On the other hand, what would that matter? She felt so good, she didn't care if everyone in Nashville saw her tonight.

"How about a nice, warm Irish coffee?" Nathan suggested.

Teeth chattering, Liz agreed, and they hurried inside.

If asked for a reason why the Opryland Hotel was so special, most people would say it was the Conservatory. Beneath a canopy of glass, story upon story of hotel rooms looked down upon a huge tropical garden.

Waterfalls splashed. Paths meandered through lush greenery. Bridges crisscrossed the man-made streams. And because of the holidays, the paradise had been transformed into an even more magical place with Christmas lights and music. As they wandered toward the bar, Liz thought it was a little like being lost in a holiday fable. At any moment she expected a group of elves to pop out from under a palm tree.

"It almost makes you believe in Santa Claus again, doesn't it?" Nathan murmured.

"My thoughts exactly." Liz paused beside a lighted gazebo and gazed up at him. "How do you always know what I'm thinking?"

"Because everything going on in that beautiful head shows in your eyes."

His voice was husky and seductive. The sound vibrated through Liz, making her wonder why she had ever thought of resisting him. Being with him made her feel free, as if the only meaningful moment in her life was the moment she was experiencing. Tomorrow she would remember that he was the conscienceless, carefree sort of man she had always avoided. But that wasn't important right now. Not when he could make her laugh. Not when he looked as if he was going to kiss her.

The idea of dancing caused Nathan to toss aside his overcoat and sweep Liz into his arms. She looked completely kissable—her cheeks still rosy from the cold, her normally perfect hair a tangle of windswept chestnut silk. But if he kissed her now, he couldn't be held responsible for what might happen next. Dancing seemed the only appropriate means of holding her body tightly to his.

So they danced. The piped-in music was Christmassy, not really conducive to dance steps. Nevertheless Nathan twirled Liz easily down poinsettia-decked walkways and across bridges festooned with garland and lights. Her cape was open, swirling about her ankles. Her head was thrown back, revealing the slender column of her throat. Her laughter mingled with the music and the subtle scent of her perfume, adding to Nathan's arousal as his body moved in harmony with hers.

They fit together well. Her head to his chin. Her soft breasts against his chest. It was easy to imagine other sultry movements, other velvet sighs and other more abandoned moments. Did Liz guess the direction of his thoughts? Nathan doubted she had to guess, especially when he ended their dance by pressing her to him, dipping her backward with a flourish that he imagined would make the dance instructor of his rebellious adolescence weep with joy.

Nathan brought her back to her feet, but their gazes remained locked. Their lips were inches apart. Her laughter died. One hand reached up to touch his hair. He held her firmly, aware of her every breath, fascinated by the way his heart seemed to be beating in rhythm with hers. What could cause that? Nathan wasn't sure. All he knew was that he had never been so in tune with another person. Not even when making love.

His head lowered, his mouth intent on the lips she parted. Then the applause started.

Startled, Liz moved away. The dance she had thought so private had an audience. A crowd of people stood in clusters, beaming at her and Nathan. From the group of nuns gathered on an elevated walkway came an entreaty for an encore. Embarrassed color warmed Liz's cheeks.

Not so Nathan. Predictably, he was bowing to the crowd, laughing as a grandmotherly type presented him with the coat he had discarded. There seemed nothing for Liz to do but drop a curtsy, too. She drew the line at an encore. The crowd dispersed and, relieved, she followed Nathan into the dark anonymity of Rhett's Saloon. But it wasn't until the waitress placed a second Irish coffee on the table that Liz's senses settled into some semblance of calm. Two drinks, she thought. Letting her hair down was getting to be a habit.

Through the crown of whipped topping, she sipped the hot, sweet beverage. "You really know how to take a girl's breath away, Mr. Hollister."

"It's my specialty," he teased, leaning forward to wipe a dollop of cream from the side of her mouth. He licked the froth from his finger, and Liz shivered at the intimacy of the action. Turning from his suddenly too intense gaze, she remembered the feel of his hard body pressed tight against hers. *Dangerous ground,* her mind warned.

She cast about for some other topic of conversation. "Maggie said she might be decorating your office."

"Eugenia says she's very good."

"Oh, she is," Liz agreed. "She did my apartment."

"I'd like to see it." His expression implied there was more he'd like to see.

Liz swallowed. He wasn't making small talk easy. "What about your apartment?" she asked. "Where did you settle?"

"In Brentwood."

"There are lots of nice complexes out that way."

He shrugged. "I'm not home that much."

"I know what you mean."

"Is your social calendar so full?"

She tried not to laugh. She had been to more parties in the last month than in the three previous months, but he didn't have to know that. Unless, of course, Aunt Eugenia had already told him. Straightforward as usual, Liz told the truth. "I'm usually working."

"Maybe you work too much," he murmured, echoing Jeannette's earlier statement.

"I don't work any harder than most people."

"But you should leave some time to laugh, Liz."

"Now you sound just like Aunt Eugenia."

"She's a smart lady," he said with a smile. "Someone with a laugh as nice as yours should use it more often."

"Having been around me for a few hours, at the most, I don't know that you're qualified to judge how often I laugh."

"Ah, but I know the signs of someone who needs a lot more laughter." Gently he touched her mouth. "Tense little lines here." His hand dropped to the fingers she had clasped around her glass. "An annoying tendency to grip beverage containers." Her hand flinched away. "And an extreme case of jumpiness," he added.

She laughed then, even though her hand wound up in his, exactly where she imagined he wanted it.

"See? Don't you feel better?" he asked. "I bet you haven't given any more thought to that case you lost."

Liz realized she hadn't. She supposed there was nothing like a hair-raising ride and a dance down the sidewalk to chase a person's troubles away. "Thanks," she said on impulse. "You did take my mind off of it."

He gave her fingers a slight squeeze, his thumb stroking across her knuckles. "People who work hard need to play hard, too."

"Is that your personal philosophy?"

"What do you think?"

She thought of his reckless abandon behind the wheel of his car and of his all-out pursuit of her. That coupled with what she knew of his professional life made him the original man on a fast track. "But you have to slow down sometimes, don't you?" she pressed.

His handsome mouth spread into a smile. His sinfully long lashes swept down over his eyes. "Oh, there are some things that I can take very slow," he whispered, raising her hand to his lips. The lashes came up, revealing a look full of sexy suggestion.

Liz caught her breath. His mouth was unexpectedly soft. Its movement against her skin was intoxicating. She knew a moment's sharp regret when he stopped and let go of her hand.

Noting her dazed expression, Nathan smiled even wider. She was a tough one, all right, but she was right on the edge of capitulation. He wondered why that knowledge didn't bring the usual surge of triumph.

Shrugging off the slight feeling of unease, he took out his wallet and laid a couple of bills on the table. "You're dead on your feet," he said, standing. "Let's get you home."

Liz was tired. So tired she gave Nathan directions to her apartment instead of bothering to go back to Eugenia's for her car. He had put the top up on the car, and she felt warm and very safe. She closed her eyes and could feel herself drifting into sleep, lulled by the hum of the powerful engine.

All too soon it seemed that they were at her apartment door. Her mind hazy from sleep, Liz didn't protest as Nathan came inside with her. She put up no struggle at all as his arms closed around her and his mouth covered hers.

It was a delicious kiss. Smooth but tingly. Like a sip of good brandy, Liz thought drowsily. Then she wasn't thinking anymore. She was moving in Nathan's arms, pressing herself to him in a complete surrender of any inhibition, letting his kiss take her to the edge of arousal. Mere kisses had never taken her so far before. She was trembling by the time he stopped. Eager for more, she brought his head back down to hers.

Nathan complied and wondered what was missing. He had her, just as he'd had many before. A few more kisses. A little more urging. He could spend the night taking her from peak to peak. For some reason, the idea had lost its appeal. He still wanted Liz—the hardening of his body told him just how much—but not for the reasons he had originally intended. He realized he had forgotten completely about her family's connections. He had allowed himself to be consumed by the pursuit of this beautiful, challenging woman. Judging by the ardency of her kisses, the chase was over.

But did he really want Liz as she was now—tired from a hard day, disappointed by the outcome of her case, more than a little tipsy? Wouldn't it be better if she were her usual sharp-witted self, if she faced him with one of her brilliant smiles, if she continued resisting just a little?

Liz moaned against his mouth and moved her body against his. Nathan knew he should have been carrying her off in search of a bed. Instead he held her away. Damn, but his reactions were so different than he had imagined. Strangely enough, he felt ashamed, as if he were taking advantage of a vulnerable woman.

So Nathan Hollister, the original scoundrel, behaved like the gentleman his grandmother had always taught him to be. He knew his father would be disappointed. But he disentangled Liz's arms from around his neck. He kissed her once more—on the cheek. Then he left.

"Dear God," he whispered, slamming his car into gear. "Please tell me this feeling isn't what I think it is."

Floating on a tide of Irish whiskey and desire, Liz went to sleep easily, dreaming of Nathan's kisses. She awakened early, and for a moment she lay staring at the ceiling, wondering why she felt so good. Memories of the night before came flooding back. She remembered pulling Nathan back to her for another kiss. She remembered him leaving. Heat streaked up her body.

"That rat. That insufferable, smug skunk. How dare he leave!"

Dazed with fury, Liz groped for her telephone and punched in a number. "Maggie," she whispered when her friend came on the line. "Maggie, dear God, the worst thing imaginable has happened."

Four

———

Maggie's breath formed miniature white clouds as she puffed along the track beside Liz. Between gasps, she said, "I'm still not sure what the problem is. Nathan Hollister is very attractive and—"

"But that *is* the problem," Liz protested, and impatience quickened her pace. She came often to the track to walk out her problems, but this morning the issue of Nathan refused to be resolved. "He's too handsome and too charming. And I almost served myself to him on a silver platter last night."

"So?"

"*So?*" In her agitation Liz walked even faster, leaving Maggie struggling to keep up. "So you know I don't do things like that, especially with people who are wrong for me."

"Maybe he's not so wrong—"

Liz's laughter was short. Maggie had been defending Nathan ever since Liz had called her. "Don't start with that again. This man is wrong, wrong, wrong. He's just toying with me, anyway. Why else did he leave?" Her hands clenched into fists by her side. "That turkey— leaving after kissing me like that."

Maggie's brown eyes widened. "Are you saying you wanted him to stay?"

"Of course not," Liz retorted, but the heat that bloomed in her cheeks had nothing to do with physical exertion. She surged forward, talking to herself. "I didn't want him to stay. He's smug, self-involved and entirely too casual about things that matter. I don't need a man like that. I don't want..." Remembering last night and how very much she had wanted him, her pace slowed as abruptly as it had quickened. "Oh, Maggie, what am I going to do?"

Liz turned, expecting some of her friend's sensible advice, but Maggie wasn't beside her. She was lying in a heap of navy-blue fleece in the grass. Liz panicked and ran toward her. "My God, Maggie, what's wrong?"

Maggie sat up just as Liz reached her. "Don't worry, I'm fine except that it isn't even ten o'clock, and you've tried to kill me."

"The only thing that will kill you is lying in this wet, cold grass."

"Then let's find a civilized environment in which to discuss this so-called problem."

The civilization Maggie sought was the cinnamon-scented comfort of her own kitchen. While Liz continued to worry aloud about the confusing emotions Nathan aroused, Maggie made coffee, toasted homemade raisin bread and listened. Liz had devoured three butter-and-jelly-drenched slices before Maggie ventured an opinion.

"I think you're nuts," she said, taking a seat at the table.

Liz blinked in surprise. Despite Maggie's defense of Nathan she had expected some support. "You're just ticked off because I forced you out on the track in the cold."

"I'm aggravated because you're being foolish."

"Foolish?"

"Yes." Maggie got up to retrieve the coffeepot from the counter. "Last week we were complaining about having no interesting men in our lives. Now here you are with a perfectly divine man pursuing you, and all you can do is complain."

"But I don't think he's divine," Liz protested.

As she refilled their mugs, Maggie sent Liz a sharp glance. "Don't give me any of that garbage. If you didn't secretly like him, you wouldn't be carrying on this way and nothing would have happened last night."

The memory of kissing Nathan brought color to Liz's cheeks again. She sank back in her chair. "Maybe you're right."

Maggie's smile was smug. "Why don't you just relax and enjoy the attention?"

"You don't understand, Maggie. The man is dangerous."

"And you can't handle him?"

The challenge brought Liz's chin up. "It's not that. I just don't want to be bothered." Maggie's response was laughter. "And what's so funny?"

"You," Maggie retorted. "You're the only woman alive who would say she didn't want to be bothered by someone like Nathan Hollister. God, Liz, sometimes you can be so high and mighty.''

Liz bristled. ''Well, thank you. It's so nice to know exactly what one of my best friends thinks of me. I bet if Cassandra were here—''

''She'd be giving you plenty of competition for the man's attention.''

''And I'd let her have him. He's the perfect man for Cassandra. They're both wild.''

Maggie shook her head. ''He might be perfect for you if you'd give him a chance. I bet he takes your mind off your work.''

''That's part of what I don't like about him.''

''You've never liked green vegetables, either, but they're good for you. You work too hard and—''

Liz rolled her eyes. ''You people are hung up on my work schedule. What's wrong? Do I look haggard or something? Well, that can be blamed on Nathan Hollister. He's the one who kept me out till who knows when.''

''Actually,'' Maggie said, resting chin in hand as she studied Liz. ''You look very good today. Very alive. I wonder if that's Nathan's fault, too?''

''Oh, for God's sake.'' Liz carried her mug to the sink. On the way she caught her reflection in the mirror over the antique sideboard. Her cheeks were rosy, and her eyes were sparkling. She looked just as Maggie had said, alive. Liz sniffed and whirled around to face her friend again. ''Don't you have any sensible advice for me?''

''Yes, I do. You should keep going out with him.''

''I said *sensible*.''

"You act as if I'm telling you to marry the man. Can't you just date him? It's Christmas, for crying out loud. You don't want a repeat of last year, do you?"

"Last year we said we weren't going through another holiday season without interesting escorts," Liz said slowly, remembering. "That was after Cassandra showed up with *two* gorgeous men on Christmas Eve."

Nodding, Maggie spread jelly on another slice of toast. "And I think Nathan is ten times more fascinating than either of those guys. At least he appears to have some intelligence."

"He's fairly sharp," Liz agreed reluctantly.

"So why not give him a chance?"

"If you'll remember, I gave him more than a chance last night, and he left."

"Which proves that he's a pretty decent guy under all that flash." Maggie grinned. "Come on, Liz, it's not the time of year to be alone. Why don't you go out with him, just for fun?"

Liz was silent for a moment, staring at the worn leather tips of her shoes, thinking of how she'd felt in Nathan's arms last night. "What happens if it gets to be too much fun?" she asked finally.

"I don't think that would be such a tragedy," Maggie murmured. Glancing up, Liz caught the wistful look on her face. "I think we both could do with a little romance."

Liz had a feeling romance with Nathan would be no little thing, but she stopped arguing. Partly because she knew Maggie wouldn't change her opinion and partly because Maggie was right about a few things—including how awful it was to be alone at Christmastime.

And if that's true, Maggie should be worrying about her own lack of interesting male companionship, Liz added to herself. But she held her tongue. When it came to men, Maggie was better at giving advice than taking it.

They dropped the subject of men altogether while Maggie took Liz to pick up her car at Aunt Eugenia's. Thankfully her aunt wasn't home, and Liz was spared the third degree about where she and Nathan had gone after the party.

On the way to her own apartment, Liz tried to decide how she was going to act when Nathan called her again. *When* he called? She assumed he would. But what if he didn't? What if Nathan had left last night because he'd decided he really wasn't attracted to her? The kiss might not have been as powerful as Liz's Irish coffee-clouded brain remembered. Forgetting she'd spent half the morning protesting that Nathan wasn't her type, Liz's heart started pounding and perspiration beaded on her forehead. What if he didn't call?

She was convinced he wouldn't by the time she arrived at home, punched a button on her answering machine and was rewarded by Nathan's smooth voice.

"Good morning, gorgeous," he said, not even bothering to identify himself. "I hope you got some rest and that you feel like going out tonight. I'm invited to another fancy party. I thought we'd have some dinner first. See you around seven, okay?"

The man's cockiness is astounding, Liz decided as she played the message again and still again. This time, however, his confidence was entirely justified. She'd be ready at seven.

For a man who had left in a panic the night before, Nathan thought he was remarkably calm as he parked in front of Liz's apartment. Calm, considering there was a part of him that still wanted to run away. The emotions Liz had aroused last night were exactly the kind he'd always run from in the past.

So why had he called her today? Why was he here now? He wasn't sure, and this indecisiveness was a new state for Nathan Hollister, who had always known what he wanted and why he wanted it. The only thing he could be certain of was that Liz was more, much more than just a stepping stone. He didn't care who she knew or who she could introduce him to. But what did he care about? Now *that* was a frightening question, and it had repeated itself all day.

Somehow he had managed to summon his usual cockiness when he had called her today. But that had been an act. Liz Patterson was one dangerous female. And she fascinated him. There couldn't be a worse set of circumstances.

Yet here he was, leaving his car, walking toward her door. Maybe when he saw her tonight he'd regain his sanity. Maybe he wouldn't want to make her laugh, or to kiss her again, or to...

"Just push the doorbell and find out," he muttered.

When she came to the door he knew he was in more trouble than ever. Liz wore blue tonight, a sexy, clinging dress almost the exact sapphire of her eyes. However, nothing, not even the diamonds sparkling in her earrings, could match the brilliance of her smile. The total effect was almost too much, and instead of the smooth opener he planned, Nathan just said, "Wow."

Mentally, Liz blessed the salesclerk who had suggested the dress. "I take it you approve, Mr. Hollister?"

Be cool, Nathan cautioned silently as he summoned a grin. "Is my approval important?"

"Well, I wouldn't want to embarrass you at your *fancy* party."

"No chance of that." He drew his overcoat closer around him and shivered. "Now, am I coming in, are we leaving, or are we just going to stand here and freeze?"

Flustered, Liz realized they were still in the open doorway. Why did this man unsettle her so? "Let's go," she murmured, picking up her evening cape and purse.

They were quiet on the drive to the restaurant. Quieter still as they studied the menus. Silence wasn't what Liz had expected given the verbal sparring in which they usually indulged. Wondering what could be wrong, she glanced over the top of her menu at Nathan. He was looking back at her. They both smiled, and Liz relaxed enough to reach for her water goblet.

"I guess it would clear the air if we just talked about it," Nathan said.

"About what?" She took a sip of water.

"About last night." He paused, grinning. "About that kiss." Liz choked, and he laughed out loud. "You remember that kiss, don't you?"

"Of course I remember," she sputtered, coughing.

"Well, I wasn't sure. You'd had a couple of drinks—"

"I wasn't drunk," she retorted.

"I'm sorry," Nathan said smoothly, looking anything but. "I didn't mean to upset you."

"I just didn't expect to be discussing this over dinner."

"Okay." He shrugged and looked back at the menu. "So what looks appetizing?"

Liz glared at him. "You can't just drop the subject now."

"What subject?"

She gritted her teeth. "The kiss."

Nathan sighed, adopted a long-suffering expression and set his menu aside. "I didn't think you wanted to discuss it."

"I don't—"

"Then why—"

"Because you brought it up," she countered, flushing with anger.

Nathan's grin grew broader. "Okay, so what did you want to say?"

"Me?" Liz asked, her voice rising. "It's *you* who obviously wants to discuss it."

He leaned forward, his hazel eyes deepening to green while his voice slid like velvet over Liz. "I just wanted to say I enjoyed it very much."

Curiously light-headed, she managed a feeble, "You did?"

"I've been thinking about doing it again."

Liz took a deep breath. *Here I go, Maggie,* she thought, *if this is what you call fun.* "I've been thinking about it, too," she replied in a strangely breathless voice.

"And?"

"It wasn't altogether disagreeable."

"Glad to hear it." Once again Liz smiled her brilliant smile, and Nathan sat back, pleased with himself. Yeah, he was in control. The secret to handling his attraction to her was to keep it light. If it got too serious, as it had last night, he'd lose his precarious footing. And he needed all the balance he could get, considering he felt like a man perched on a cliff's edge with the enemies at his back and nothing but a frayed rope between himself and safety. A frayed rope was better than none, however, and Nathan set out to be his most entertaining.

As they talked, Liz began to enjoy herself. They argued a bit about politics, of course, but they agreed on many other subjects—such as movies and favorite sports and sixties rock music. They even shared a piece of chocolate mousse cake in relative peace, although Nathan insisted to the end that Liz had taken more than her share.

She couldn't totally relax, however, especially not when they headed for the party. In the restaurant with people surrounding them, it was easier to push aside thoughts of last night's kiss, to smile and flirt when Nathan said he'd enjoyed it. But in the dark, close confines of his car, that kiss and the possibility of more simmered between them.

By the time they got to the party, she was tense and nervous and irritated with herself. The way she was behaving was nonsensical. She was a grown woman, a person with some sophistication, not an innocent encountering her first bona fide charmer. It was time she got a grip on herself, but that was easier said than done. Especially when she spent so much time wondering how Nathan's tawny hair would feel beneath her fingers.

It didn't help that the party was given by Hugo Mantooth, the man for whom Nathan had directed the winning campaign against Jim Levinson. She didn't like Mantooth or most of his cronies, and although the guests included others Liz knew and liked, she wasn't enjoying herself.

Nathan fit right in, however. Liz retired voluntarily to the sidelines and watched as he worked the room like a pro. He played the power game very well, using his charm to turn a social occasion into an opportunity to promote himself. This side of him was at odds with the man who had danced with her last night and teased her this evening at dinner. Which side was the real Nathan?

Pondering that, she studied her barely touched glass of champagne and frowned. Nathan's deep voice brought her out of her reverie. "You don't look as if you're enjoying yourself." When she shrugged, he set her glass on a nearby table and took her hand. "Let's blow this joint."

"Do you leave every party early?" she asked after they'd said their goodbyes to the host and hostess.

"You're a bad influence on me." He pulled her toward the door. "Besides, I think I know something that will be a little more fun."

"Don't tell me—skating instead of dancing or maybe a roller coaster ride instead of a drive?"

His smile was mysterious. "Just wait and see."

So it was that Liz soon found herself standing in a park, braving the cold with dozens of others. Instead of dancing she was singing a Christmas carol. Beside her, the man who had recently been shaking hands with some of the state's most noteworthy politicians was belting out "Deck the Halls" in a reasonably good voice. Instead of champagne, he held a cup of hot chocolate. The sight didn't mesh with his sophisticated, witty persona, but he looked as if he was having a wonderful time. It occurred to Liz that Nathan always seemed to be enjoying himself—no matter what the occasion.

While those around them swung into another song, he spoke close to her ear. "You're still too serious-looking, Miss Patterson. Don't you think this is fun?"

Not trying to make her answer heard over the swell of voices, Liz merely tucked her hand in the bend of Nathan's elbow and raised her voice in song. Just like last night, she felt completely liberated. In the last twenty-four hours she'd had more fun than she'd had in ... in longer than she could remember. Maybe everyone was right in saying she had been working too hard. How good it felt to laugh, to feel as if nothing mattered but remembering the words to a song and flirting with the handsome man at her side.

They stayed and stayed, laughing and singing with perfect strangers until Liz's feet were frozen in their stylish but impractical pumps. The magic of the evening didn't desert them, however; it followed them straight to her apartment and sent her into Nathan's arms as soon as they had closed the door behind them.

If he was surprised that she made the first move, he gave no sign. He kissed her back, the kind of slow, pulse-stirring kiss Liz remembered dreaming of the night before. He tasted of chocolate and the cold. He smelled like a man, a hint of spice, a splash of musk. She liked the scent, liked the faint scrape of his beard against her skin and the warm feel of his hand sliding under her cape and across the cool silk of her dress. Her pulse quickening, she moaned his name against his mouth.

Not knowing or even caring if that was a sound of encouragement or protest, Nathan kept on kissing her, kept on touching her. One hand was on her back, urging her closer. The other raked with controlled impatience through her silky hair. His lips slipped from her mouth and down the side of her neck. Sweet and fragrant and warming to his touch, her skin was the kind a man wanted to taste. Giving in to the impulse, his kisses became nibbles. Each one was rewarded with her tiny gasp of pleasure. That sound stirred him more than any touch, and his body reacted, hardened. Groaning, he captured her mouth with his again.

Responding greedily to the not-so-gentle pressure of his lips, Liz's tongue curled against his. The feeling sent arousal spiraling down her body with the speed of a falling star. She twisted her mouth under his and thrust herself against him, frustrated by the layers of clothing separating them. She wanted him close...*closer. As close as a man and woman could be.*

Having admitted to that deep desire, Liz's few remaining inhibitions scattered. She pushed at Nathan's bulky overcoat, her hands eager for contact with his hard, male muscles. Last night those muscles had bunched beneath her hands while he had danced her down the Opryland Hotel sidewalk. Last night she had felt his strength when he had swept her backward. Last night he had kissed her just like this.

Last night.

Liz's face grew warm as she remembered the night before. Was it really just last night? That meant two nights in a row she had stood here with Nathan. Two nights she had kissed him, allowed him to kiss her until she was damp and aching for his most intimate touch.

Two nights in a row. So fast. Too fast.

This wouldn't do. Wouldn't do at all.

"Nathan," she murmured, pulling away. "Nathan, I think we have to—"

"Oh, no, you don't." His voice had a rough edge, as if forcing it from his lips was an effort. "Don't think. Just kiss me." His mouth nibbled at hers, eating away her resistance.

Liz surrendered to the delicious taste of him before pulling back once more. "Nathan, we can't just keep on—"

"Who says?" Like a flame, his tongue licked at her lips, parted them, burned his way into her mouth. When he had kissed her so thoroughly that Liz could only want him to continue, he drew back, whispering, "Why can't I just keep on kissing you?"

"Because kisses become something more," she protested when she could speak again. "And I'm not—"

"Not ready?" he completed for her. "Ready for what?"

She swallowed, fascinated by his passion-clouded hazel eyes. "We're going too fast," she managed to say.

His chuckle was low and deep, as sexy as his kiss. "You lawyers. You're always trying to anticipate the other guy's next move. I just want to kiss you, Liz." His hand stroked across her cheek, thumb trailing along her jaw. His touch was so slow, so deliberate, so welcome. "Can't I just kiss you, Liz?"

He's like a kid begging for a taste of icing with his eyes on the whole cake, Liz decided. And dammit, she should know better than to offer him a crumb. But she did, anyway, lifting her mouth to his, kissing him until the world spun round and round in shades of green and gold, like the colors that mingled in his eyes.

Finally it was Nathan who ended the kiss. *Take it easy. Keep it light,* he told himself. His arms still around Liz, he settled her head against his shoulder and brought a handful of her soft, sweet-smelling hair to his face. He let it slide through his fingers and breathed in her aroma, content just to hold her while the desire pounding at his body eased. He knew that if he had any sense, he'd set her away from him and walk out the door.

His mouth curved into a wry smile at the thought. Walking away wouldn't help. He had proven that last night. He would just come back and be more fascinated by Liz than ever. Though how he could be any more intrigued he couldn't imagine.

When his pulse at last returned to its normal pace, he straightened away from her. "Know what I'd like to do?"

Afraid to hear the answer, Liz automatically wiped a smudge of her lipstick from his chin. He caught her hand and held it against his cheek. The gesture was unexpected and oddly touching. "What?" she whispered. "What do you want?"

He grinned. "Maybe a cup of coffee?"

"Coffee?"

"Or some brandy?" Still smiling, he brought her fingers to his lips. "Then maybe we can sit on the couch and kiss some more."

"That sounds very nice." She slipped her hand from his. "In theory."

"Liz, do you have something against good ol' American necking?"

She couldn't help but laugh. "Considering what has just transpired in this hall, I can't believe you have to ask that."

"But you must," Nathan insisted, suddenly serious. "'Cause kissing you is all I want to do." To his complete amazement, he meant every word of what he as saying. There wasn't anything he'd rather do than spend the next few hours cuddling with Liz. Well, he amended, maybe there *were* a few hundred things he'd rather do, all of them involving Liz and something more erotic than cuddling. But for tonight, just to kiss her, to hold her, to make her laugh, for tonight that seemed almost enough. As for the rest of it—well, all in good time. *All in good time.* He made that a promise to himself.

Liz studied him a long, silent moment before shaking her head in wonder. "You mean everything you're saying, don't you?"

His smile peeked out again. He might as well be honest. "At least I mean it for tonight." She sighed and rolled her eyes, and he rushed to defend himself. "Is it so impossible to imagine that I just want to get to know you?"

"Getting to know someone means different things to different people."

"I mean it in its most innocent sense. Getting to know each other is usually why people date."

"Date?" Liz raised a skeptical eyebrow. "Do people still date, Nathan? I thought they just started relationships."

"Come on," he cajoled. "Why don't we stop standing here in our coats, arguing over the terminology?" Not waiting for her to agree, he slipped off his coat. "Let's at least get comfortable if we're going to fight."

Liz was going along with his plan before she quite knew it. But she and Nathan didn't argue. Instead she made some popcorn. He poured some brandy. Together, they settled on her couch, turned on the television and watched Bing Crosby and Danny Kaye sing and dance their way through *White Christmas.* During commercials they did some more old-fashioned necking.

Nathan was sweet, as charming as ever, and he never once made the move Liz was expecting. If anything, she was the one who held on to him a bit longer than was absolutely necessary when he finally said good-night.

The next morning as she slipped into her favorite sweater-dress, Liz felt as unbalanced as she had the day before. Dammit, why couldn't Nathan behave as the unprincipled rake he had appeared to be at first? But no, he had to keep surprising her. Champagne one minute. Hot chocolate the next. Playing politics with the power brokers. Then singing Christmas carols in the cold. Holding her. Just holding her. God, she could get used to that.

Remembering the feel of his arms around her, Liz spent half the morning staring blankly at the files she'd brought home from the office. When the doorbell rang, she had to fight the urge to run to answer it. As she expected, Nathan was on the doorstep. His hair was adorably disheveled, his cheeks red from the cold, and he did things for a fisherman's knit sweater and tight corduroy jeans that no man should be allowed to do in public.

"Hello, gorgeous," he said and kissed her. Hard. Very direct. A kiss full of promises. He left her breathless, and then asked in the calmest, most unaffected way, "Ready for brunch with Eugenia?"

Eugenia. Liz almost groaned, thinking of her aunt. How in the world was she going to hide from Eugenia how utterly, completely besotted she was with this man?

Damnation. A smug, I-told-you-so speech from her aunt was the last thing she needed right now.

Five

———

Peering into the back seat of her car, Liz counted colorful, beribboned baskets. "One...two...three." She grinned at Nathan. "Three more stops and we're finished."

"Are you sure you don't have a couple dozen more in the trunk?"

"Well, if you're up to it—"

"No, no, that's fine," Nathan said quickly and started the car. "Where to now?" For all he knew Liz might really have other baskets hidden away, but he thought twenty-odd deliveries were enough for one day. It was now after three o'clock, and they had spent the day delivering holiday food to some of the neediest clients Liz's office had represented this year. Liz had organized the project, and though everyone in the office was supposed to be helping, she had made the lion's share of the last-minute deliveries with Nathan's help.

She found the address of their next stop on her list and sighed. "I wish I had a couple of thousand more baskets and plenty of people to help get them out. What I'm doing doesn't even make a dent."

Nathan had to smile. Perhaps delivering some food to a few dozen families was small potatoes in a city the size of Nashville, but it was only part of what Liz did for others. In two short weeks, he had learned a great deal about her generosity. Aside from her charity work, she gave money to every street-corner Santa and bell-ringing volunteer, all in addition to her job, where she put her finely trained legal mind to work for a fraction of what she could earn at one of the city's top firms.

She could have her pick of positions. Last weekend Nathan had escorted her to the bar association's Christmas party. Liz seemed to know every prominent judge and attorney in this part of the state. The fact that her father had retired from the bench meant something. However, from the compliments given to Liz about a variety of cases, she seemed to have earned her colleagues' respect. All she had to do was ask, Nathan thought, and they'd hire her in a minute.

But instead of power lunches and partnership conferences, she was defending petty thieves and prostitutes. And delivering Christmas baskets to their families to boot.

Her enthusiasm for everything she did was the amazing part. That enthusiasm endowed her with phenomenal powers of persuasion. She had convinced him to help her instead of leaving for Memphis to spend Christmas Eve with his grandparents. Although he had to admit he would have been very disappointed if she hadn't asked him to stay. He was going to Memphis tonight after dinner with Eugenia.

Liz's voice broke into his thoughts. "What are you smiling about?"

"Christmases past," he replied evasively. He thought of last year, visiting his grandparents, sitting beside a warm fire and savoring the mellow taste of whiskey-laced eggnog. For some reason delivering baskets in the cold with Liz was more appealing than that familiar, pleasant routine. She did that to him, made him do things and think thoughts he'd never contemplated before. In a short space of time, Liz had affected him deeply. He frowned, pondering the ramifications of that admission.

Liz had turned serious, too. "I'm sorry, Nathan. I guess this isn't your idea of holiday cheer. If you'd rather go home, I can do the rest on my own."

"Don't be silly. I'm glad to help."

She eyed him with suspicion. "Are you sure?"

Nodding, Nathan guided her car to a stop in front of a rather ramshackle house. "Besides, you don't need to be alone in some of these neighborhoods."

Liz laughed. "This is Nashville, not New York. I'm at home here."

Glancing from her brilliant smile to the house's sagging porch, he murmured, "Yeah, sure, you look right at home." Basket in hand, he followed Liz up the cracked sidewalk.

A woman opened the door. Her face was lined, but whether from age or suffering it was impossible to determine. Her eyes were dull. Like broken windows in an empty house, Nathan decided. He had seen that look in many eyes today.

The woman brightened a bit as she recognized Liz and asked them to step in from the cold. Inside, two girls who could be no more than three or four sat on a shabby sofa, watching an old black-and-white television set. There was none of the just-controlled excitement Nathan would associate with Christmas Eve in a house where children lived. The house was cool. It smelled of onions instead of evergreen.

Liz introduced Nathan and presented the basket. "Mrs. Bartlett, I hope this will make your holidays more enjoyable."

"You shouldn't have," the woman protested. "You've already done so much for my Peggy."

Peggy Bartlett. Nathan put the names together and remembered the young woman whose trial Liz had been so upset about losing. This must be Peggy's mother.

"I hope your daughter will be home for next Christmas," Liz murmured, her gaze resting on the children, who smiled shyly in return.

"Yes, well . . ." With a pessimistic shrug, Mrs. Bartlett managed a smile. "I hope so, too. The girls miss their mother. They don't understand where she is."

Liz knelt so that she was level with the children. "Are you two excited about Christmas?" They nodded eagerly and proceeded to name several toys they wanted. Nathan caught the pained expression that crossed their grandmother's face. He followed her gaze to a tiny plastic tree and the pitifully few packages underneath. It was a sure bet Santa wasn't bringing everything on these children's lists. A glance at Liz's face showed Nathan she was thinking the same thing.

She was silent as they left the house and headed toward their next delivery, and when she spoke, he realized he'd been waiting for her words. "I have to do something for those kids."

Nathan shook his head. She just never stopped. "Liz, you've already done something for them. Thanks to you, they're going to have a good meal."

"But I want to do more."

"I'm sure there'll be someone else looking in on them, a community church or someone who'll bring some presents. I bet they'll have a better Christmas than lots of kids."

"They won't even get to see their mother," Liz murmured, as if she hadn't heard him.

"And you imagine that's your fault, too." It was a statement and not a question because he had begun to understand how she thought.

Liz bristled defensively. "I was her lawyer."

"Did you do the best possible job on the case?"

"Of course, but—"

"No buts," he cut in. "If you did everything you could, then you have no reason to feel guilty."

"I don't feel guilty," Liz snapped. "But Peggy isn't a criminal. She just gets involved with the wrong men."

"Her mistakes. Not yours."

"But that doesn't change the fact that her two children are spending Christmas without her. The least I can do is make the holiday a little nicer for them."

Nathan heaved a frustrated sigh. "You can't change the world, Liz."

"I'm not trying to. But when I see someone I can help, I do it. It's just not in *my* nature to walk away, Nathan."

"Are you implying that walking away is *my* nature?" he demanded, his voice full of controlled fury.

Liz shrugged, and with a quick motion and a muttered curse, Nathan pulled the car to the side of the street. "I don't think I deserve that," he said tightly, turning toward her.

"Because you spent the day distributing food to the needy instead of seeing and being seen by the right people?" Liz taunted. Instantly she regretted the words.

"I'm not looking for a medal," Nathan said, his eyes narrowing. "I came today because I wanted to be with you. I never pretended otherwise. Now I have to admit I've gotten a good feeling from what we've done. But I'll also admit I don't share your zealousness. I don't think that makes me someone who deserves remarks like you just made."

Liz was silent, her head bowed, feeling more than a little ashamed of herself.

Sliding his hand under her chin, Nathan lifted her face. "I do care," he whispered. "If you audited my checkbook, you'd find I give something to those who aren't as fortunate as I am."

Liz bit her tongue, not saying how she usually felt about those who demonstrated their concern with only money. In her opinion the only way to make a real difference was to give something of yourself. But that was *her* opinion. It was small-minded to think everyone should share it. Maybe if Nathan weren't becoming so important to her, she wouldn't want him to think just as she did. And maybe that meant he was becoming too important. Like Peggy Bartlett, she might just be involved with the wrong man. But if he was wrong, she didn't know why he made her feel so right.

"I'm sorry," she murmured, touching Nathan's cheek. "I shouldn't have said what I did. I got carried away thinking about those kids waking up tomorrow in that cold house with none of the things they asked for waiting under that tree." She took a deep breath. "But it isn't your fault, and you didn't deserve what I said."

The tight set of Nathan's mouth relaxed. "Apology accepted." He touched his lips to hers in the lightest of kisses, and with eyes full of an emotion she couldn't quite fathom he scanned Liz's face. "Until I met you, I didn't think unselfish people really existed."

"Maybe I'm just selfish in a different way." *I could learn to be selfish where you're concerned,* she added silently, shaken by the strength of that notion. She held her breath, waiting for him to react to the emotions that were surely apparent in her eyes.

But Nathan had turned away to start the car. "What do you say we deliver these last two baskets and then head for the mall?"

"The mall?"

He grinned. "Yeah, to find a toy store. We have to play Santa Claus, don't we?"

If Nathan had really been looking for medals, he thought Liz's smile would have been enough. The way she kissed him while they stood in a line at a crowded toy store was a bonus.

But then a kiss from Liz felt like a prize, an unexpected reward, given for an achievement he didn't know he was striving for. For two weeks he had been kissing her, two hectic, wonderful weeks that had passed like minutes.

Together they had stopped, wrapped packages and decorated her tree. They had even, though Nathan couldn't believe he had participated, decorated Christmas cookies in Maggie's country kitchen. With Liz on his arm, he had dropped in on more holiday parties than he could remember and been introduced to dozens of important people whose names and faces he filed away for future reference. Old habits died hard, Nathan decided, even though the people he had met were secondary to the pleasure of being with Liz.

Each time before seeing her, he told himself to keep it light. And each time he forgot his own advice. He wanted her more than he had ever wanted any woman. No, that wasn't right. He couldn't even think of Liz in the context he had thought of other women. His reactions to her were too complex and not yet fully understood. He knew only one thing for certain: this was much more than sexual desire. If sex had been the issue, he felt sure they would be lovers.

For Liz wanted him. He could feel it in her kiss, in the way she trembled when he touched her. But he hadn't pushed. Though patience had never been Nathan's finest virtue, he found he could be patient for Liz. She was worth the wait. In fact, he was enjoying taking it slow, wooing her, discovering her mind before he explored her body.

She was bubbling over with excitement after they delivered the toys to a rather tearful Mrs. Bartlett. On the sidewalk outside the house, Liz threw her arms around Nathan. "Thank you for helping me. I don't think I could have enjoyed my Christmas if I'd thought those little girls weren't going to have a nice one."

"It was fun," Nathan replied, kissing her nose.

Liz studied him thoughtfully. "Mr. Hollister, you never stop surprising me."

Though his tone was teasing, there was unmistakable tenderness in the way his fingers brushed across her cheek. "Surprises keep things interesting, although I can only hope to keep a smart girl like you guessing for a few months, at the very most."

His reference, however casual, to a future that encompassed more than just the next day made Liz pause. Though they had spent a great deal of time together, she had no idea where she stood with him. Every time she began to think something important was happening between them—as it had today—he laughed and backed off. Maybe someone to laugh with was all he wanted. And wasn't that okay? she asked herself. When Maggie had encouraged her to go out with him, the idea had been to have a good time. Liz should have known it would go deeper than that for her. Their first kiss should have told her that. And if Nathan really wanted to keep it casual, how could he kiss her in that heart-fluttering way of his.

The cold wind rustled through a pile of dried leaves as he brushed a tendril of hair from her face. "Are we going to stand here while you try to think of something to say, or can we get in the car? If we don't get this show on the road, we're going to be late for Eugenia's shindig."

"It isn't a *shindig*," Liz insisted. "It's a quiet family Christmas Eve."

"Eugenia said there'd be plenty of people there."

"Neighbors and good friends like Maggie and her brother and Cassandra." Groaning, Liz looked down at her jeans and then headed for the car. "Good Lord, I'd forgotten about Cassandra. I've got to go home and make myself gorgeous."

"For Cassandra's benefit?"

"You'll understand when you see her."

But Nathan didn't understand. That evening he stood at one end of a crowded room and studied Liz and her two friends. Clustered near the Christmas tree and wearing bright holiday clothes, they made a pretty picture. Though they were all different types, they were all attractive women.

Cassandra was flamboyant, with a cloud of black hair, flashing dark eyes and a curvy figure she displayed to its best advantage in an abbreviated red dress. Her dramatic style was in definite contrast to Maggie's warm, blond loveliness. But Nathan thought Liz's cool, classic style outdid them both.

"They're like a trio of beautiful jewels, aren't they?"

Eugenia's quiet voice drew his attention from the three friends. Then he glanced at them again, nodding in agreement as he sipped his champagne. "And Liz is the most brilliant. She shines from within."

Chuckling, Eugenia placed a hand on his arm. "It's nice to hear you appreciate my niece's finer qualities."

"Which is what you intended I do," Nathan retorted.

"Even the best of intentions sometimes go awry." The tiniest of frowns touched Eugenia's brow as Maggie brought her much-older date forward to say goodbye to Eugenia.

When they were gone, Nathan murmured, "Matchmaking not going well?"

"Merely stalled, my boy, merely stalled," Eugenia said. "But to get back to Liz—"

"I knew you would." He suppressed a grin.

But Eugenia was dead serious as she continued, "Liz sparkles so brightly because she has many facets, all of them deep."

Setting his drink down on a nearby tray, Nathan completed the comparison as he knew Eugenia wanted him to. "You mean she's like a truly beautiful diamond."

"You're very perceptive," Eugenia said soberly, still watching her niece. "There are times when I wish she weren't so deep, that she cared just a little less."

Nathan looked at Liz, too. She was now perched on the arm of Cassandra's chair, one hand on her friend's shoulder, but she was talking to Maggie's brother, Daniel. Her pose was that of a peacemaker, her beautiful face very serious. A person didn't have to know her to see how much she loved these people. Daniel walked away, and Liz watched him with obvious concern, the same concern she'd shown this afternoon for two children she barely knew. She was a special woman, and Nathan wondered why she put her heart on the line so often. As he had learned from his father, love hurt.

To his surprise, anger curled through him as he thought of the many times Liz's impetuous heart had probably been bruised.

His next words to Eugenia came out harshly. "I'm not going to hurt her, if that's what you're worried about."

The older woman shook her head. "Oh, Nathan, people hurt each other. That's inevitable in all but the most casual of relationships. The thing you can't forget is to appreciate her." Her lips curved upward in a smile. "Treat her as any precious jewel should be treated. Admire her. Very often and up close."

Leaving her seat by Cassandra, the subject of Nathan and Eugenia's conversation strolled toward them. "Okay, let's hear it," Liz demanded. "What are the two of you up to?"

Eugenia drew herself to her full height. "Really, Liz, must you know all my secrets?"

"You never tell me any of them."

"Then ask Nathan." The older woman glanced over Liz's shoulder and frowned. "Now, if you'll excuse me I really must go speak with Maggie. I can't imagine why she wants to go out with someone old enough to be her grandfather."

Laughing, Liz and Nathan watched her bear down on an unsuspecting Maggie, who was now sitting alone by the fire.

"Eugenia's going to have to accept that not all her plans work out," Liz said.

Nathan took her hand and lifted it to his lips. "Some of them do."

"Perhaps." Liz had hoped to sound aloof, but as always, the feel of his warm mouth against her skin scattered her composure.

Nathan let his lips linger on her hand, savoring her subtle perfume, enjoying the flush that stole into Liz's cheeks. If he kissed her pretty mouth right now, that heat would flood through her. He'd be able to feel it no matter where his lips chose to wander.

Imagining the warmth of skin he had yet to touch, desire tugged at him with insistence. It was all very well to be patient, but there were moments—such as now— when he wanted to back Liz up against a wall, to push his hands under her red and black spangled sweater, to place her hands on him, to watch every inch of her slender, fragrant body flush pink with excitement. After he had pressed himself into her softest depths, he wondered if she would be able to look at him with such cool blue eyes.

Appearing to sense the direction of his thoughts, Liz tugged her hand free and glanced toward the window behind them. "I heard someone say it's going to snow tonight."

"Don't place any bets. How many times has Tennessee seen a white Christmas?"

"It could happen," Liz insisted. "And you're driving to Memphis."

"Interstate all the way. I'll be there in under three hours, even if it snows."

"But your grandparents will be worried."

Nathan laughed. "My grandparents stopped worrying about me twenty years ago. That's how they've made it to such a ripe old age." He caught Liz's hands in his again. "If I didn't know better, I'd think you were trying to get rid of me."

"Of course not." A tiny voice inside her added, *I don't want you to go at all.* But she ignored that and summoned a smile. "I haven't even given you your present."

"How about now?"

The room was still crowded with neighbors and friends. It was entirely too public. "Let's go outside," she suggested impulsively. "If it's going to snow, I want to see it begin."

After finding his present under the tree and making sure Eugenia was absorbed in Maggie, Liz led Nathan through the kitchen. Jeannette was taking a tray of canapés from the oven. She regarded Liz and Nathan with surprise.

"Are you leaving, *chérie*?"

"Just looking for some privacy," Nathan said smoothly, an explanation that caused Jeannette to beam with pleasure.

Once they were on the kitchen's tiny side porch, Liz grumbled, "I guarantee she's reporting our whereabouts to Aunt Eugenia right now."

"Who cares?" Nathan brought her close for a very hard, very thorough kiss. "Umm, I think I just got my present."

Liz hid the package she was carrying behind her back. "Then I'll take this back."

"Not a chance." In seconds, he was tearing the wrapping paper off with the enthusiasm of a child. A mahogany-encased clock soon glinted in the light streaming from the kitchen windows.

"I hope it's okay," Liz murmured, suddenly anxious about the gift. It was a valuable antique, but now it seemed too impersonal. Yet what else did you buy a man you had been seeing a scant two weeks, even if you felt as if you had known him forever? That admission made her even more nervous, and she rambled on, "Maggie said it would look perfect in the office she's putting together for you, and I—"

"She's right and thank you." Setting the clock on the shelf under the window Nathan silenced her with another kiss. But that did nothing for Liz's nerves. If anything, it made them worse, and she shivered.

She rubbed her arms. "It's freezing out here. Maybe we should go back—"

"Not until you open this." The square black box he offered caused Liz to swallow. The name of an exclusive jewelers was emblazoned in gold across the top.

"Nathan, you shouldn't—"

"Open it before you say anything."

Almost holding her breath, Liz obeyed. A gold pin, crescent-shaped and crisscrossed by a narrow stripe of diamonds winked at her. "It looks like my earrings," she murmured.

"You wear them a lot. I looked for something to match."

"You went to a lot of trouble," Liz said. She glanced back at the pin. "It's just beautiful, Nathan. Thank you." She stepped into his arms, shivering again and not from the cold. God, but she didn't want to feel this way, all warm and trembling and yearning. She didn't want to need this man. When had she let herself fall for him?

"Turn around," Nathan whispered.

"What?"

"Just turn around."

It had begun to snow. Showers of snow fell thick and fast in the glow from the floodlights near the driveway. Forgetting the cold and laughing with pleasure, Liz drew Nathan off the porch and into the yard. "Christmas snow," she said as the flakes melted against her skin. "The best kind of magic."

Maybe magic was the source of the tingle Nathan felt as he gazed at Liz. He thought he could stand here in the cold all night, just watching the delight on her face. But the snow was falling fast and already clinging to the grass and the asphalt of the driveway. He had to leave now, just in case they really did have a white Christmas.

"But you can't leave," Liz protested. "The roads might be bad."

"The only bad thing would be disappointing my grandparents." Nathan brushed some snow from Liz's hair. "We're not close, but I won't let them down."

This glimpse into Nathan's feelings surprised Liz. He never said much about his family. In fact, she knew little more about his past than she had the first night they'd met. She had to remember to ask Eugenia about his grandfather. But that could wait. Right now she just didn't want him to leave.

"I know you have to go," she whispered, turning on the step of the porch. Nathan stood beside her, his expression unreadable in the snowy shadows. "I wish you could stay." She brought his face down to hers, underscoring the words with her kiss.

He drew back, framing her face between his hands. "Now I know how sailors feel when they're leaving for months of duty at sea." He kissed her again. "And I know why they come home."

Realizing she was indeed holding on to Nathan as if he were leaving on a perilous journey, Liz stepped back. She should behave like a woman with a modicum of maturity instead of a silly clinging vine. "I'm sorry, I know you have to go. It's just Christmas and—"

"And if I didn't *have* to go, I'd be taking you up on the offer you made with that kiss." His voice was rough as he pulled her back into his arms.

"Nathan, I didn't mean—"

"Yes, you did. A woman only has one thing in mind when she kisses a man the way you just kissed me."

Liz threw caution to the wind, tilting her head at a cocky angle. "You must be used to kisses like that. Otherwise, you might be tempted to stay."

"Oh, sweet J—" The words were lost as he crushed his mouth to hers yet again. And while he kissed her, his hands were everywhere. They tangled in her hair and brushed across the hardening tips of her breasts before settling on the curve of her bottom as he fitted her body to his. His hips pressed hard against hers, and Liz was assured of how very tempted he was to stay.

"Okay," she murmured when she could talk. "I believe you."

"I'll be back day after tomorrow."

"Why does that seem so long?" Liz asked, admitting more than she'd intended about her feelings.

Nathan rested his forehead against hers. "I don't know, but it does." He chuckled. "Maybe I'll come back tomorrow."

With those words and the memory of his kiss to buoy her, Liz almost floated back into the house. Nathan said his goodbyes to Eugenia and to Maggie and Cassandra, who were the only remaining guests. The snow was falling harder when Liz stood beside his car, kissing him goodbye again. She watched until his taillights disappeared down the drive. Then she squared her shoulders and went back inside, expecting a firing squad of questions.

From her seat beside the fire, Cassandra got off the first shot. "Okay, Liz, you sneak, where did you find that luscious man?"

Liz dropped onto the sofa next to Maggie and ignored the question. She didn't want to talk about Nathan right now. All she wanted was to curl up and remember the deep sound of his voice and the way the snow had caught in his ridiculously long, dark lashes. Only Eugenia's presence kept her from stretching like a lazy, well-satisfied cat. So far, her aunt hadn't done much smug posturing about the amount of time Liz was spending with Nathan. She could only hope the trend continued.

"Nathan is just a friend." With elaborate unconcern, Liz brushed a hand through her slightly damp hair. She frowned at the giggle Maggie tried to smother in her wineglass.

"Let me tell you something," Cassandra drawled in her Southern, honey-dipped voice. "A friend who can send you back in here looking so very well kissed is a friend worth hanging on to. Has he got any brothers?'' Maggie giggled some more.

With a glare for her friend, Liz turned to Eugenia. ''Well, go on, you might as well add your opinion, too.''

Rather haughtily, Eugenia rose from her chair. ''Liz, dear, you know I wouldn't interfere in your love life.'' The three younger women exploded with laughter, but Eugenia's dignity was marred only by the twinkle in her eyes. ''Merry Christmas, my darlings. I'm going to bed.'' Head held high, she swept from the room.

Still laughing, Cassandra kicked off her red pumps and curled her legs under her. ''Now we can really talk. Liz, I want to know everything about this Nathan Hollister.''

''If you can believe it,'' Maggie told her, ''Liz didn't like Nathan very much at first.''

''Oh Lordy, Liz, I always did say you had more brains than sense.''

''And statements like that are why I always said you had neither,'' Liz retorted, tossing a pillow in Cassandra's direction.

''Oh, stop throwin' things and give me the dirty details—all of 'em. Does he kiss as good as he looks?''

''Cassandra!'' Liz admonished. ''Why is it you're still asking the same questions you asked when we were sixteen?''

Eyes open innocently wide, Cassandra tossed her pretty head. ''Can I help it if I knew at a young age what was important about a man?''

''That's right.'' Maggie sipped her wine and looked at Liz. ''So, why *don't* you tell us exactly how Nathan kisses?''

"You've been drinking again," Liz said sternly, stealing the glass and sipping it herself. "You're acting as silly as Cassandra."

"Now is that a nice thing to say about someone as sweet as Maggie?" Cassandra demanded. Tapping a perfectly manicured red fingernail on her chair's arm, she studied Liz in silence for a moment. "I do believe you like this one."

Liz allowed herself a smile. "I do believe you're right."

"Which is the best thing she's said about any man in more than a year," Maggie added.

Frowning a little, Cassandra continued, "You've surprised me, Liz. He's not what I would have expected."

"And why is that?"

"Well, you always go for these leather-elbowed, corduroy jacket kind of intellectuals. Nathan seems a little...umm...slick."

"More your type?" Liz suggested, grinning.

"You could say that, yes."

"Uh-oh," Maggie cautioned. "Better watch out, Liz."

"Oh, for heaven's sake," Cassandra protested. "I would never try to bird-dog a man belonging to either of you."

"Nathan doesn't belong to me." Setting the empty wineglass on the end table, Liz stretched.

Maggie laughed. "Famous last words."

Cassandra was still frowning. "I'm still surprised, Liz. It's hard to see a man like Nathan helping with one of your causes."

"Not every man I date has to be a social worker, does he?" Liz demanded, although Cassandra's remark made her think of the disagreement she and Nathan had had this afternoon. They *did* look at the world in different ways.

"Eugenia told me he's an extremely ambitious man," Cassandra continued.

Liz shrugged. "Is there something wrong with ambition?"

"No, but you've never liked the self-serving type."

"Oh, come now," Maggie interrupted. "I don't think Nathan is exactly *self-serving*."

Realizing that was exactly how she had once characterized him, Liz said nothing.

Cassandra, however, grinned. "I guess it all comes down to spontaneous combustion."

"What?" Liz and Maggie said together.

"Well, if you rub two opposites together, you do get sparks."

Liz chuckled dryly. "Cassandra, I think you have your scientific theories mixed up."

"Well, you were provin' some theory all night," Cassandra retorted, arching an eyebrow in Liz's direction. "We probably could've started a car on the electricity you and Nathan generated this evenin'."

While everyone laughed, Liz decided there was some truth in Cassandra's teasing. She and Nathan were opposites in many ways. Perhaps that was why she found him so exciting. But if that were true, it also stood to reason their sparks would eventually burn out. What happened then? Liz knew herself well enough to know she wouldn't escape without some damage to her heart.

It's already too late for that.

The warning whispered along her nerves, even as she glanced at the mantel clock. Nathan hadn't been gone half an hour and she was missing him. She bit her lip, almost tasting his kiss. She took a deep breath, imagining she smelled his tangy, masculine scent. God, she was going nuts. She had to get a grip on herself.

Looking up, she found Cassandra and Maggie staring at her. "What?"

"Lordy, Lordy," Cassandra murmured. "This is more serious than I thought, Maggie. Liz is already staring off into space."

"Maybe we should call the state patrol," Maggie suggested. "They could probably intercept Nathan and bring him back."

"Just stop it," Liz demanded. "I think enough has been said about me and Nathan for one night. Cassandra, don't you think you ought to be going home? Did you stop by to see your parents on your way from the airport?"

Cassandra shuddered ever so slightly. "Oh, Liz, don't even mention Mother and Daddy. They are so mad at me—"

"What is it this time?" Liz said, not a bit surprised. Cassandra's parents were always furious with their daughter.

"Well, for one thing, I had used up all the interest on Granddaddy's trust fund by August—"

Maggie cut in, "And what else is new?"

"But they also don't believe that I've really and truly found what's going to be my life's work."

As if on cue, Maggie and Liz settled deeper into the sofa's cushions, groaning. Cassandra changed careers with each new phase of the moon.

"But listen, you guys," she pleaded. "This time I'm really sure. Let me tell you . . ."

With half her mind on Cassandra's latest scheme, Liz looked at the clock again. It was after midnight. If Nathan were as good as his word and came back from Memphis tomorrow night, she could see him in twenty-one . . . maybe twenty-two hours. How many minutes was that? she wondered, calculating in her head.

He had her counting the minutes.

She was lost.

Utterly lost.

She felt that way until the next night when Nathan appeared at her door, exactly twelve hundred and sixty-five minutes from the time she'd started counting.

Give me strength, she prayed, lifting her lips to his. Just enough strength to stay out of this man's bed for a little while longer. Just until she was sure of why she wanted to be there.

Six

___

Her mind on the case she had just handled, Liz made her way through the crowded corridor outside the courtroom. This case had been a simple one. Though he had asked for the representation of an attorney, her client had admitted his guilt in an assault on the manager of his apartment building. She had plea bargained with the district attorney's office for the lightest sentence possible. Because her client had no prior record, he had gotten off easy. Open and shut. Simple.

So why wasn't she satisfied. Maybe it was why her client said he had attacked the man. That made her wish the person who owned the building had been on trial.

But why should it matter so much to her when she had a full case load and a million other things to worry about?

Frowning, Liz started to glance at her watch when a hand took her wrist and pulled her to the side. A deep voice spoke low against her ear. "Don't struggle, counselor. That'll just make it worse." Alarms jangled along her nerves.

Then she heard the chuckle.

"Nathan," she murmured, twisting around to face him. "You scared me."

"Hey, I'm sorry," he replied, with a look that wasn't really contrite. "I thought you'd recognize my voice. What's wrong? Got your mind on some important case?"

"They're all—"

"—important cases," he finished with her. "Why is it I knew you'd say that?" Sliding his hands up to her shoulders, he smiled the slow, sexy grin she had come to know so well. His smile was as arousing as his kiss. Or his touch. Or his voice. To be honest, she had to admit everything about him made her think of tangled sheets and velvet touches and release. Sweet, final release. Lately it seemed as if that release was all she thought of.

"Nathan," she said again, forcing her voice past the tightness in her throat. "What are you doing here?"

"I had an appointment nearby. I was hoping for lunch with my best girl."

"Oh, are all your other girls busy?" she teased.

With his thumb, he brushed the corner of her mouth. The gesture was quick, no more than a butterfly's touch, but the desire to open her lips and taste his skin almost overwhelmed Liz. She had to close her eyes and concentrate to keep from sliding down the wall.

When she looked up, Nathan's smile had faded. "I don't have any other girls," he whispered, leaning forward until their mouths were inches apart. "You know that."

"Yeah. I know that."

They stood unmoving for a long moment, saying nothing, their eyes speaking volumes. The surrounding crowd simply fell away until the request of a man needing to pass broke the spell.

Looking around as someone awakening from a dream, Nathan moved out of the way. "Can you have lunch?"

Feeling disoriented, Liz glanced at her watch. "I've got a meeting I have to make in ten minutes."

"Then I'll walk you to your car."

"The meeting's upstairs."

"I guess I'm just out of luck, huh?"

Grinning, not looking at him, she made a great show of straightening one lapel of his overcoat. "Maybe someday your luck will change."

He caught her hand. "Count on that." The words were a promise. She nodded. "How about dinner?"

The question was rhetorical. She and Nathan had dinner together almost every night. "Let's not go out. I'll pick up something on the way home. Can you make it at seven?"

Nathan nodded and dropped a kiss on her forehead. "I'll bring the wine. Go have a good meeting."

How very domestic we sound, Liz thought as she walked away. She turned halfway down the corridor, hoping to catch another glimpse of Nathan's tawny hair. The crowd parted, and she saw that he hadn't moved. He was watching her. Even from this distance, she didn't have to imagine the smoldering look in his green-gold eyes.

That look kept her preoccupied throughout a dull meeting and the long hours of a dreary January afternoon.

Weeks ago Liz would have said it was impossible for two consenting adults who desired each other to wait as she and Nathan were waiting. Based on what she had seen of his impatient nature, it was downright alarming, especially since she wanted him with a fierceness she had never dreamed possible. But they were waiting, drawing it out. That heightened the tension.

There had been a couple of men in Liz's life. She knew what passion was. She had played the sexy game of tease and touch and tantalize. But this waiting, this yearning for Nathan had taught her something new about arousal.

Maybe it wouldn't be so intense if physical attraction were all they had. But there was more, much more. Funny, but until Nathan came into her life, she hadn't noticed how black and white her existence had become. There'd been her work, her friends and her family, but something had been missing. Color, she decided. Nathan had added color to her days. He made her laugh. He listened. He seemed to care.

So why didn't they stop this nonsensical circling of each other and act their ages?

"Why indeed?" she muttered to herself as she stood in line at the grocery store. Idly her gaze scanned the magazines on the rack by the checkout counter. From the cover of a woman's magazine a caption jumped out at her, "The Lost Art of Seduction." *Lost art, my foot,* Liz thought, picking up the magazine. Her skills might be a little rusty, but she knew something about seducing a man. Nevertheless she flipped through the magazine's glossy pages. Maybe seduction was what Nathan needed.

Warm air and delicious aromas enfolded Nathan as Liz opened the door to her apartment that evening. It feels like coming home, he thought as he kissed her. She was soft and fragrant, exactly the sort of welcome he thought he could get used to.

"I'm honest-to-goodness cooking," she said, taking the bottle of wine while Nathan automatically hung his overcoat in the closet. *Just as if it belongs there,* he realized, and stood staring at the by-now-familiar clutter in Liz's hall closet. Damn, but he was getting comfortable here.

"Nathan?" He looked up to find her studying him in a thoughtful way. "Bad day?"

"No, no, not at all."

"Good. Then come out in the kitchen and open this wine. I need it bad." She turned, and he wondered if it was his imagination or if her slender hips wiggled more enticingly than usual in her black stretch pants. Maybe it was because he had been thinking of the gentle curve of those hips . . . thinking of nothing but Liz ever since he had seen her at noon.

He couldn't see her without wanting to kiss her. He couldn't kiss her without wanting something more. After what had happened between them on Christmas Eve, it had been difficult, but he had clung to the charade that they were just going out, that nothing serious was developing between them. He was afraid of what he'd have to admit if their relationship took its next logical step. Becoming Liz's lover might leave him vulnerable to a world of hurt, the kind he'd sworn he would never endure.

But damn, how he wanted her.

"Nathan?" Liz called from the kitchen, and he loosened his tie, although his neck wasn't the part of his anatomy that had tightened.

"Steady," he muttered to himself. "Remember to keep it light."

He paused in the doorway to the dining alcove that opened off the kitchen. The candles on the table definitely weren't his imagination. Neither was the sparkling crystal or the silver-rimmed china or the fresh flowers or the sexy beat of the jazz playing on the radio.

In the kitchen, Liz took a pan from the stove and turned around. Her oversized white sweater slipped from one shoulder, revealing smooth, glowing skin. "Dinner's ready. I hope you're hungry."

His eyes on her naked shoulder, Nathan nodded.

"I'll get some wineglasses," she added. On her way to the cabinet, she brushed past him and her sweet scent filled his head.

Drawing a deep, rather shaky breath, Nathan took the glasses she offered and put them on the counter.

"The corkscrew's down here." Liz bent over and dug through a drawer that was halfway to the floor. Nathan turned and his groin collided with her soft, tantalizingly rounded derriere.

The contact immobilized every muscle in his body.

Every muscle, that is, but one.

Liz stood and started to turn away. The movement brought a strangled command from Nathan. "Don't."

"But what—"

"Don't move," he muttered, clamping his hands on either side of her hips. "Don't even think about moving." He pressed himself ever so slightly against her.

The motion made Liz catch her breath. "Nath . . ." The word dissolved into a sigh as his mouth descended to her uncovered shoulder. Warm and pleasantly moist, his lips opened against her skin, and the corkscrew in her hand clattered to the counter.

"So sweet." His voice danced through her. "So very sweet." Eager to feel his mouth against hers, she tried to turn around.

"No," he whispered as his hand moved with excruciating slowness up her hips and under the sweater to her bare skin.

Sparks, Liz thought while his touch lingered on the skin just below her breasts.

Combustion, she added when that touch slid upward to her hardening nipples.

With her breasts pebbling against his palms, Nathan buried his face in her hair. "Oh, Liz, you feel..." He searched for a word, any word to describe the sensations that were tumbling through him. It was impossible. Nothing had ever felt like this.

Liz arched her back and raising an arm, trailed her fingers along his cheek. His hands lifted her breasts, and her sigh stretched into a moan of pleasure. Instinctively he ground his hips against her. He grew harder, heavier, and willed himself to hang on to his control.

"Nathan." His name had never sounded like this before, equal parts plea and caress.

She succeeded in twisting in his arms this time. His hands fell away from her, and their lips met in something that was more explosion than mere kiss. Absorbing the impact all the way to the soles of his feet, Nathan stepped backward.

Liz took advantage of his movement to slip her hand between their bodies. *So much heat,* she had time to think before he pulled her hand away.

"Not a good idea," he murmured in a ragged voice.

"That's up to me." She tipped her head back to look into his eyes. "Because I'm seducing you."

"I would say it's the other way around, wouldn't you?"

"You just got a little ahead of me, that's all."

"A little?" He grinned and deliberately brought her hand back to the juncture of his thighs.

"Nathan," she whispered, her eyes widening.

"Is that approval or shock?"

"Nathan," she repeated, her voice dropping to a husky level. Her hand stayed where he had placed it.

Tunneling through her hair, his fingers held her still while his mouth plundered hers again. Tension built inside Liz, a restless yearning for his touch. As if on cue, his hand strayed back to her breast. Then he grunted in frustration.

"This has to go," he said, tugging her sweater upward.

Liz had never expected to feel shy. That just wasn't part of her plan for tonight. Nonetheless, as her sweater was tossed aside, her eyes fell under Nathan's regard.

With strokes light as down, he traced a line from her throat to each breast. "Oh, Liz. You're beautiful." Before she could react, he lifted her to the kitchen counter. Her gaze met his, surprised and perhaps a little outraged.

"Nathan!"

"Sh," he whispered and then placed a kiss on her breasts. First one, then the other. Quick kisses. Then lingering. *Blossoming roses,* he thought as each coral-rimmed tip puckered for his attention.

Lost to the sheer abandon of the moment, Liz thought time itself ground to a halt. Want zigzagged through her, arcing downward, focusing in the deepest core of her femininity. Her need was so tangible she could taste it. Restlessly she moved against Nathan. His lips strayed from her breasts up to her mouth, and she roused herself enough to fumble with his tie. It fluttered to the floor, and she concentrated on his shirt. Haste made her hands shake.

"Too many damn buttons," she muttered. Then the material parted, and her hand slid over the muscles of his chest. His skin was warm. It grew warmer still as her fingers raked through the crisp whorls of tawny hair. Her thumb flicked across one flat male nipple. Nathan jerked in reaction.

He caught her hand. "Liz, if you don't want to be taken right here and now, on the kitchen counter, don't do that again."

"Maybe we should move to the bedroom."

"I hope I can walk."

"Maybe this will inspire you." Wondering at her audacity, Liz slipped from the counter. Slowly, her eyes holding Nathan's, she peeled off her form-fitting stretch pants. Beneath them she wore only a filmy bit of black and red material, a little something she had tucked away for just such an occasion.

His gaze shifted downward and lingered so long on the panties' lacy front triangle that Liz lost her nerve. "Don't you like them?"

"Yeah." He pulled her hard against his chest. His voice was a growl against her throat. "But I'm gonna like them better when they're off."

Later, Liz could never recall exactly how they got to her bedroom. But she remembered everything that came after.

The sheets were cool. Nathan wasn't. On his skin was the salty gloss of perspiration. Liz found the taste oddly exciting. More exciting was the way he tugged her panties downward with his mouth. She wondered at his control as he touched her. Over and over. With his hands and his lips and his voice. His words reached her in places a mere physical touch could never have gone. They inflamed her, sent her into the inferno once and then again.

And still he wasn't inside her.

"Please," she whispered, reaching for him, opening her legs in invitation. She was full of sensations, but she felt empty without him filling her, moving with her. "Now, please."

Nathan didn't know where he found the strength to be gentle, but some hidden reserve of control came to his aid. With infinite care he drew Liz beneath him and fitted their bodies together.

The first velvet thrust brought her hips upward and pulled him deeper than he'd intended.

On the second, he forgot gentleness and stopped counting.

Minutes—or was it hours?—later, Liz curled her body next to Nathan's side. "I'm speechless," she whispered.

He chuckled and pushed a damp tendril of hair from her forehead. "There's a first time for everything, counselor."

"It isn't a first. You've been getting the last word since the very beginning. I think that's what infuriated me the most about you."

"Were you infuriated?" His fingers traced the outline of her lips. "We've come a way since then."

She sighed. "A long way. Very fast."

This time he did more than chuckle.

"What's so funny?"

"It doesn't seem fast to me," he answered, his tone sobering. "In fact, it feels like we waited forever to get to this point."

"Six weeks," Liz said. "I've known you only six weeks, and look at us. I don't usually do things this fast, Nathan."

"Sure you do."

"I beg your pardon?"

"If you see someone who needs your help, you jump in, feet first." He kissed her, and she could feel his lips slanting upward in a smile. "Why don't you just think of me as one of your needy cases?"

"Needy?" Her hand dipped low across his stomach. "I don't think you need anything right now."

"Don't be so sure." To her surprise, he stirred at her touch.

"You're insatiable."

"I'm starved for a woman's touch."

"Okay." Giggling as she tossed back the covers, Liz straddled his lean hips. "How's this?"

"Good for a start."

She leaned forward, her hair falling like a silk curtain on either side of her face. The curling ends skimmed across Nathan's skin, more arousing than a kiss. Catching the strands in one hand, he let them slip through his fingers. The feeling was indescribably sexy. He had imagined being with Liz like this ever since the first time he'd seen her. The moment was worth waiting for.

"This isn't how it usually is for me," he murmured, brushing her hair back from her face.

"So you're not always terrific in bed?" she teased.

He grinned. "Of course I am. That's not what I meant."

"You mean you don't usually wait this long to sleep with a woman you desire?"

He paused at her bluntness. "You cut right to the heart of matters, don't you, counselor?"

"I'm not a fool, and believe it or not, I've dated a few men of your type in my day." She slipped back to his side and pulled the sheets up around them both. "So tell me, why did you wait this time?"

Nathan turned on his side, facing her, settling one hand on the curve of her hip. How natural that felt. "You're different."

"That's not much of an explanation."

He swallowed and decided to be honest. "Liz, you're the kind of woman who demands things from a man. Promises. You're all or nothing. I knew that from the beginning, but I kept coming back."

He heard her take a deep breath. "I've never been a person who can be casual about anything."

"No kidding," he muttered, his voice harsher than he intended. "Commitment is your middle name, while it's never even been in my vocabulary. I guess that's why you scare the hell out of me."

Liz went very still. His words weren't exactly what a woman wanted to hear from her lover.

He broke the silence. "I'm trying to be honest—"

"And I suppose I should appreciate that." She sat up, tucked the sheets under her arms and turned on the bedside lamp. Pushing the tangled hair out of her eyes, she faced Nathan. "What are you trying to tell me about us?"

He blinked in the light and pushed himself up, but the only sound was the scrape of his hand rubbing across the faint stubble on his jaw. Liz's mouth went dry. If commitment wasn't his style, then they didn't have a future, and all she could expect was what they had right now. Dammit, why did she have to want so much more?

"Liz," Nathan murmured, touching her shoulder. "I really don't know exactly what I'm trying to say. But this isn't . . . you aren't what I planned on."

"What did you plan? A quick, easy affair? I'm not like that Nathan."

He sighed. "I already told you that I know that. I knew that from the beginning. That's why it wasn't supposed to get this far."

"This far?" Liz repeated uneasily. "You make what's happened between us sound like a mistake."

"No, it's not a mistake, but it isn't what I originally intended, either." He paused and took a deep breath. "At first you were just convenient."

"Convenient?" Anger began to churn through Liz as she jerked away from the hand he'd put on her shoulder.

And too late Nathan realized his attempt to be completely honest had been a complete miscalculation. But he plunged on, trying to explain. "It's not like it sounds, Liz. But at first, before I really knew you, I thought you'd just be a good contact, someone—"

"—who'd get you invited to the right parties?"

"Yes . . . I mean . . . no," Nathan corrected as genuine fury sparked in her eyes. "I know it sounds terrible now, but I had this idea of using you—"

That sent Liz from the bed. She jerked a robe up from a nearby chair and tied the belt with quick, furious motions. "Nobody uses me, Nathan."

"I know," he said lamely, getting up from the bed. God, he had messed this up but good, but he had to try to salvage it. He had to make her understand how his feelings had changed. "Liz, I found out you weren't anyone I wanted to use. From the first time we really talked, I knew you were more than a stepping stone. Then when I kissed you..." He paused, remembering that first electric kiss. "That scared me to death, Liz, because I knew right then how much you were going to mean to me. I knew you wouldn't be like any other woman I've ever known."

Hearing his words but not taking in their meaning, Liz looked away from Nathan and closed her eyes. He had set out to use her. She should have guessed. She should have known better. From the beginning she'd had him pegged as a carefree, careless sort of man. A selfish man. But then he had kissed her, he had done a few unexpectedly sweet things, and she had let herself fall for him. And now he was going to break her heart. His only redeeming point was that he was doing it now, before she got any more involved. God, but she had made a mistake. That made her even angrier.

"Tell me something," she demanded, stepping closer to him. "Does anything really matter to you? Anything aside from your work?"

Nathan frowned at her. "Of course. I *care* about you. That's what I'm trying to tell you."

"Oh, really? That's not how it sounds to me."

He bit back a curse. "Liz, you've got to listen to what I'm telling you. I care about you. That's why I'm here with you now. You're making me want the kind of things I never wanted." He touched her arm. She tried to jerk away, and he hauled her around to face him. "Please, I know I started out with the wrong intentions, but that's all changed. I don't know where what we have now will lead—"

"Especially since users don't commit to anyone but themselves," she cut in scathingly.

"Liz," Nathan began, reaching for her hand. "I wish you'd listen to me, believe me."

"And I wish I could understand what kind of person doesn't want commitment. Maybe I'm a fool, but I don't understand. Are you just going to spend your life alone?"

He tried to choose his words carefully. "That never seemed to matter. My father—"

"Yes, your father," Liz said with a bitter laugh. "Where does someone like you come from, anyway?"

"That's not important."

"Oh, but it is. It might explain why you're such a cold bastard."

This time the curse exploded from Nathan. He turned from Liz and started looking for his clothes.

The wounded look on his face drove the anger from Liz. God, why hadn't she held on to her temper long enough to listen to him? "Nathan, please," she said now. "I'm so—"

Nathan closed out the words. Tightening the reins on his anger, he pulled on his slacks and spoke in a cold, controlled voice. "Okay, Liz, since you're so eager to hear it, let me tell you about my father. Or maybe I should start with my mother. She married my father for his money. Only he really didn't have any. All he had was a big old house with a good address and parents of his own who spent their days just a little mystified as to where all the money had gone. I really wish Dad had told Mother all that before he married her. But he waited. She didn't figure it out until I was born. And that's when she left. For good."

Nathan jerked on his shirt and chuckled mirthlessly. "Poor old Dad. He never got over her leaving. And he spent his life trying to make money. I guess he thought if he rebuilt the family fortune, she'd find out about it and come back or some such nonsense. And of course she never did, and Dad never made much money, either. He..." Nathan laughed again. "Now you talk about cold bastards, Liz. That's exactly what my father became." He paused, his eyes widening as if he'd made a huge discovery. "So I guess you're right, I'm just my father's son."

Liz was regretting that remark more with every passing moment. "I'm sorry," she said.

"Yeah, me, too," Nathan muttered, reaching for his belt.

"Nathan, please don't leave." He couldn't walk out, not after what had happened between them, not before she could make him see how sorry she was. "Please." She saw Nathan hesitate. "I'm sorry. I wasn't listening to you. I guess I've been so sure you were going to hurt me that—"

"Liz." Dropping his belt to the floor, Nathan came back to her and gathered her close in his arms. "God, the last thing I ever want to do is hurt you."

"Then why did you say I scared you?"

"Because, dammit, you do." He gave her shoulders a little shake and pulled back. "I tried to tell you. You've got me thinking seriously about that dirty word."

"Commitment."

"Yeah. That one." He brought her close again. She smelled so good, like flowers and sex. And he needed her. Much as he hated to admit it, he needed her in his life. "Liz, what I was trying to tell you is that you make me feel like good relationships are possible. I never felt like that before.''

She touched his hair. ''Because of your parents?''

He shrugged. ''I guess so. It just never looked to me like people got much out of pledging themselves to each other.''

Liz drew away, her gaze searching his face. ''They were just one couple. It doesn't have to turn out that way.''

''Really? I guess I've just had the wrong friends. I don't know too many people who stay together.''

''But Nathan, just look at your grandparents. They must have been married fifty or more years.''

''Bad example,'' he muttered, his mouth tightening again. ''Grandfather has always liked the ladies. Even now. Grandmother has just suffered in silence. I don't condone what he does, but I also don't understand her acceptance.'' He shook his head. ''I care about them both, but they're hardly the perfect couple.''

''Oh, Nathan.'' Liz hugged him hard, as if that contact could take away all of his hurts.

''I guess I'm a pretty bad risk,'' he said, and then gave a shaky laugh. ''You know, people ought to come with an explanation of their risks—like dangerous products do.''

''Huh?''

''Maybe it should be more like a case history. People could carry it around on cassette. And when you met someone, you'd just pop it in the stereo and then decide if you even wanted a second date.''

''Then no one would ever go out more than once,'' Liz retorted. ''Because we've all got problems and imperfections and things in our past that have affected us.''

"Really?" He drew his finger along her jaw. Slowly. Almost reverently. "And what're yours? You seem pretty damn perfect to me."

"If I were perfect, we wouldn't have just had this blowup. I would have listened to you."

He kissed her then, a kiss such as they'd never shared, flavored with melancholy. But as always, it made her want him. She drew him backward with her.

"Liz," he murmured against her neck. "My sweet Liz."

The words made her smile. "*Your* Liz."

"Too possessive for you?"

She shook her head. "But you have to prove it." With a smile, she untied her robe and let it drop to the floor.

"Gladly." He pulled at the buttons to his shirt, then shrugged it aside and stood to shed the pants he had pulled on so impatiently.

Liz curled up on the edge of the bed, watching him. In the light from the lamp, his hair glinted gold. On his chest. On his thighs. Between them. Catching her breath at his sheer male beauty, she reached for him. He quivered at her touch, and she surrendered to a purely wanton impulse to press her lips to the skin just below his navel. Her reward was his sharply indrawn breath. Then he drew her upward till she kneeled on the bed, her face inches from his.

"I'm going to try," he promised in a fierce whisper. "I'm going to try with you, Liz. You're the first woman I ever thought was worth the attempt."

"That doesn't say much for your choice of partners, Mr. Hollister."

He leaned closer, his breath caressing her skin. "Maybe I was just waiting for you."

She had no chance to analyze the words. No chance at all since he was kissing her, touching her. He wasn't slow this time. He was almost inside her before they fell back on the bed, and his long ever-deepening strokes left no room for Liz to think about anything but pleasure.

They finally ate dinner at midnight, and Nathan spent the night with her. Liz didn't try to analyze that, either. She just enjoyed being held in his arms and waking up beside him when her alarm clock jangled early the next morning.

He stayed the next night, too.

And the next.

Nathan could feel himself becoming entrenched, fitting into the routine of Liz's life as easily as his coat fit in her hall closet. By the weekend, he had a toothbrush hanging beside hers in the bathroom. He pondered the significance of that for about a minute. Then he forgot it.

There were just too many other things to think about. Such as going to work on a new image for a client. Or hiring an assistant. Or touching the stars with Liz in his arms. He concentrated on the bits and pieces of life and ignored the overall picture.

It was better that way, he decided. Because what was happening between him and Liz still, quite literally, scared the hell out of him.

And what, he wondered, did that say about their future?

That was another question he chose to ignore.

Seven

The corridor was dingy, filled with the stale odors of food and cigarette smoke and as cold as the outdoors on this early February afternoon. Liz stood uncertainly at the bottom of a flight of steps, half expecting someone to materialize from the shadowed corners. "What nonsense," she murmured, and started upstairs.

The handrail was solid beneath her hand, a contrast to the squeaking stairs. A month ago, however, the railing had been broken. It hadn't been repaired until Marissa Lockhart had fallen from the stairs to the hall below, and her father had vented his frustration by attacking the man who managed the apartments.

A person who didn't know the facts might label Roy Lockhart a troublemaker, especially since he was an under-educated, often unemployed man, whose wife, a waitress, provided the main support for the family. Liz could forgive the man his rage, especially when she considered what might have happened to Marissa.

She thought the real culprit in the situation was the man who owned the building, Claxton Summerfield. You couldn't blame a manager for the owner's neglect, and all of Summerfield's apartment buildings seemed to be in similar disrepair. He was always within the law—if only just. His buildings passed inspections—barely. Legally he couldn't be forced to do anything more than he did now.

The Lockharts couldn't even sue him over Marissa's injuries. The question of why a three-year-old had been playing alone on the stairs blew a hole through that plan, and a crew had repaired the stairs the very afternoon she fell. His company had paid all her medical expenses and had agreed to pay for the physical therapy or operations she might need in the future. But in Liz's eyes it still wasn't good enough. The next time repairs were postponed, someone could be killed. Before that could happen, she wanted to do something about improving the quality of life in Summerfield's buildings.

As she reached the second-floor landing, a door opened to her right, and a short, slender woman greeted her. "Come on in. I've been watching for you."

The apartment matched the corridor in shabbiness, but Cheryl Lockhart had used green plants to make it as cheerful as possible. With her husband in jail and three children to support, Cheryl could have been forgiven for losing hope, but hard luck had yet to rob her brown eyes of their optimistic sparkle.

"Where's Marissa?" Liz asked. On her other visits to the Lockhart home, the child had been ensconced on the sofa, her broken arm and leg propped up by pillows.

"My neighbor's got all the kids," Cheryl explained. "Somebody's sick at work, and they called me in a little while ago. I can use the hours."

"I'm sorry, we could have met tomorrow."

"I got time yet, and I knew you wanted this quick." Cheryl handed Liz a sheet of paper. "Some of the men helped me, and we went over all three buildings. I hope it's what you wanted."

The list of problems ranged from falling ceilings to broken windows and ineffectual heating. None of the improvements listed could be considered luxuries. Moreover, the tenants were willing to do much of the work themselves if Summerfield would supply the materials. Liz had made that suggestion at a tenant's meeting last week, and it had been accepted with no argument. For the most part, she had found the people living in these buildings to be accommodating. They didn't expect favors, and they wanted to earn their own way. She was determined to show them they could make changes by working within the system.

"This is exactly what I need," she told Cheryl. "What I'll do now is write Mr. Summerfield a letter, asking him to make these repairs. Maybe knowing an attorney is involved will get us somewhere."

Nervously, Cheryl twisted her hands in the apron of her waitress uniform. "You don't think he'll be mad, do you?"

Liz smiled in reassurance. "Mad about what? We haven't done anything to make him mad—yet."

"But we might have to?"

"Maybe." The other woman frowned, and Liz studied her thoughtfully. "Are you worried about him being angry?"

"Well, if he kicks us all out, it won't be easy to find another place we can afford."

"He's not going to kick you out. You pay your rent, don't you?"

"Yeah, but—"

"Then don't worry," Liz replied and glanced at her watch. "I've got to go, Cheryl. Is that car of yours running, or do I need to give you a lift to work?"

After dropping the woman off, Liz was already fifteen minutes late for dinner with Nathan. She was half an hour behind schedule by the time she hurried into their favorite restaurant. She found Nathan at a cozy table near the window.

"You look like you just ran a marathon," he said, and then caught her to him for a brief but hard kiss.

Liz, who had been feeling drained, was warmed by his welcome. Smiling, she sat in the chair he pulled out for her and gave her drink order to a hovering waiter. Then she apologized for being late. "I had an important appointment."

"More important than me?" Nathan teased.

"Is that impossible to imagine?"

"Nearly." His hand slid over hers. "I'd be tempted to think it was another man except that I recognize the avenging angel zeal in your eyes. Who are you rescuing this time?"

Perhaps he didn't intend to be flippant, and under other circumstances, Liz might not have taken it that way. But she was tired, and the comment set her teeth on edge. "I'm so glad my little crusades amuse you," she muttered before pulling her hand away.

Nathan caught it again. "Hey, I'm sorry. I wasn't making fun of you."

She sat back in her chair and took a deep breath. "And I didn't mean to overreact. It's just been a long day."

"For me, too." He squeezed her fingers. "We've both been going at it full tilt for the last couple of weeks."

"And getting almost no sleep," Liz added softly.

Nathan answered with a slow, secret, lover's smile.

Elbow on the table, she rested her chin against her palm and returned the smile. "I think what we need is a few days alone, away from the craziness. Somewhere out of town."

"Sounds good. How about this weekend?"

The waiter arrived with her drink, giving Liz time to mentally flip through her appointment book. "This weekend's out. Saturday is Maggie's birthday. What about the next weekend?"

"Sorry. I've got a client coming in from out of town." Nathan reached in his jacket for his pocket calendar and opened it. "Let's see, two weeks from now...no, that's no good, either."

Digging out her own calendar, Liz went through the weeks. They had eliminated eight consecutive weekends when she started laughing. "Would you look at us? If ever there were two people who didn't have time for a relationship, it's us."

"But we seem to be having one," Nathan reminded her.

"Even without weekend getaways."

He brushed his knuckles across her cheek, and his voice deepened to its warmest, most intimate level. "We could always barricade ourselves in the apartment for . . . say . . . a day and a night?''

"Surely we can find that much time."

"And I can bring some champagne."

Liz moistened her lips, aware that Nathan followed the movement of her tongue. "I could get some Brie and some of those chocolate-dipped strawberries you like so much." She grinned. "And maybe some whipped cream?"

"This is sounding better and better," he whispered. His eyes were slumberous, half shielded by their dark, curling lashes.

His eyes alone can seduce me, Liz thought, and wished they were at home instead of in a crowded restaurant.

"You want to leave?" His husky voice startled her.

"You're reading my mind again."

"Okay, let's . . ." Nathan's gaze focused on something over her shoulder, and he mumbled an "Excuse me" before standing. "Senator," he said, extending his hand to a man who was about to pass their table.

Liz blinked. How could he switch gears so quickly?

The state senator Nathan had stopped acted pleased to see him. So pleased, Liz thought the man was going to sit down with them after he had been introduced to her. However he went on his way after a few minutes but not before asking Nathan to call him and set up an appointment. "I've been hearing some good things about you, Hollister. We definitely need to talk."

Once the man was gone, Nathan sat down, murmuring, "Talk about luck."

Lucky for whom? Liz almost asked out loud. She was feeling rather resentful herself. But rather than say something she'd probably regret, she picked up her drink.

"He could be making a run for Congress next year," Nathan continued, still looking toward the door through which the man had disappeared. "I wouldn't mind having a piece of that action."

"Won't you be handling Hugo Mantooth's campaign again?"

"By the time the election rolls around, I expect to be handling more than one political client. Especially if I can put some of my competitors out of business."

"Feeling cocky tonight, aren't we?" Liz murmured.

His smile was cold. "It's kill or be killed."

The unapologetically ruthless tone of his voice sent a chill down Liz's spine. In her mind, she saw lights winking out at PR firms all over the southeast. She swallowed another sip of her drink. "You should have been a hired gun. The CIA could probably use someone with your temperament."

"I believe the same could be said for you."

She looked up in surprise. "What?"

"Doesn't it take a killer instinct to be a good attorney?"

"In a way, but—"

"But that's different, right?" Nathan drawled, a sarcastic edge to his voice.

Liz rose to the bait. "Yes, in some cases I do think it's different."

"Then I guess we just disagree, don't we?" As quickly as it had come, the sarcasm left his voice and his mocking half smile gave way to a grin. "And weren't we doing something much more interesting before we got into this discussion?"

He changes so easily, Liz thought again, even as he smiled into her eyes. It was as if all he had to do was slip from one mask into another. Who was the real person underneath? As intimate as they had become, she still couldn't answer that with complete certainty. He had warned her that opening up to another person wouldn't be easy for him, and certainly, with his family he hadn't learned any of the benefits of sharing himself. But Liz wanted him to be different with her. As yet, however, she hadn't made much progress. She was falling in love with a man she didn't really know. Now that was frightening.

"Where were we?" he asked, breaking into her thoughts.

"I think we were going to order," Liz lied, picking up her menu. Staying in this crowded restaurant seemed as imperative now as slipping away with him had seemed earlier. If they were alone now, she would push him for answers and explanations. *And I don't want that,* she told herself with something akin to panic, *because I might not like what I learn.*

What happened? Nathan wondered more than once during dinner. One minute Liz had been warm and loving, eager to be alone with him. The next, she was distant and quiet, even wary.

At her apartment she said she had work to do. He thought she wanted him to leave, but he felt just obstinate enough to stay. He undressed and climbed into bed with an article he needed to read. In gown and robe, she got in beside him, spreading file folders like a wall around her. Except for the rustle of turning pages and the scratching of pen against paper, the room grew silent. Ominously so, Nathan thought.

When he could stand it no longer, he sat up and pulled a folder from Liz's hands. "Okay, so why don't you tell me what's wrong?"

"Nothing," she retorted, grabbing at the file he held just beyond her reach. "Now stop being silly and give that back."

"Tell me what's bugging you and I will. Otherwise..." He waved the folder. "Otherwise, I'll have to dispose of this."

"Nathan, don't be childish—"

"Childish?" he taunted, grinning. "Did you say childish?"

"Nathan—"

"How's this for childish?" He tossed the folder toward the ceiling. Even though it was too heavy to go far, papers fluttered all over the bed before the major portion landed with a thump on the floor.

"Damn you, Nathan." Snatching up papers, Liz started out of bed. "What a mess."

He tossed back the covers and scrambled across the bed toward her. Folders spilled their contents onto the bed and the floor. "Forget the mess. You're not moving until I find out what's bothering you." He hauled her toward him.

"Nathan, look at what you're doing," Liz protested, trying in vain to get away. "These are important."

"If you don't want them messed up, then don't bring them to bed with us," he growled as he tossed those papers he could reach onto the floor. Then he cut off Liz's escape by pinning her down with the weight of his body. Her lips were very close, too tempting to resist, even though he wanted to talk to her. So he kissed her.

"Nathan!" Liz pushed at his bare chest. "Now stop it! You've got to straighten up this—"

He caught the rest of what she was trying to say beneath his mouth. Her struggles grew a little less insistent.

"Nathan." This time his name was fainter, and her lips opened under the pressure of his.

"Now that I've got your attention," he whispered. "What's wrong?"

Her only answer was to urge him closer, her arms twining around his neck.

It was his turn to pull away in protest. "Liz, I want—"

"Just shut up," she whispered. "Shut up and kiss me."

He needed little encouragement. His mouth slanted across hers, and desire, urgent as always, pushed aside all other thoughts. His hands were working at the sash of her robe before he realized his own intent. The robe fell open, and the ivory satin gown she wore beneath was soon pushed to her waist, the matching panties stripped away.

She looked impossibly lovely, spread across the bed, her slender thighs open to his gaze. The abandoned pose made him harder than any touch. Yet he had to touch her, and the creamy skin of her legs was warm against his hands. Like silk and fire, he thought, mesmerized by the sensation.

With her whispered invitation soft against his ear, his fingers slipped upward, inside the velvety folds of her most secret self. She gasped at the first stroke. Then he found the budding center of her passion and felt the shudder that ran through her body. He circled the nub again and again, teasing her. When her hips began to move against his hand, he pressed his lips to the pulse beating at her throat. The taste of her skin was sweet, like the floral scent of her perfume. Lost in that fragrance, he stilled the movement of his hand, and she whimpered in protest.

"Nathan, please—"

"Please what?" he mimicked, chuckling. "Please don't crush your files?"

"No...please don't..." Lightly his fingertips brushed along her inner thigh, and she drew a long, shaky breath. She brought his hand back to her, pushing upward. Her words came out in a rush. "Please don't stop."

"If you insist." Intent on her pleasure, he stroked her, his touch at first gentle. Then more insistent. Harder. Until her hands dug into his shoulders and her breath came in harsh gasps. She arched against him, her body rippling in climax. Once. Then once more. He felt every wave of her release, so excited by the movement of her body and the emotions washing across her face that he ached from the heaviness of his need.

That exquisite pain demanded assuagement, and while she still trembled, he slipped inside her.

Her sapphire eyes, blurred by passion, opened halfway. "No," she whispered. "This way." Quickly, still scattering loose papers with every move, she pushed him onto his back. The robe fell from her shoulders as her movements pulled him deeper. So deep. So tight and moist and warm. Though she rocked against him, he resisted the pull, held back the threatening overflow.

"Slow...slower." His voice sounded as strained as the iron clamps he had placed on his control. "Let's make it last."

She slowed her movements, but with each thrust of her hips, the straps of her gown slid down her arms. The bodice slid with them, until the very tips of her breasts peeked over the satin edge, tantalizing Nathan. He could actually feel the way those pert bits of flesh would pucker against his tongue.

When he could stand the imagining no longer, he pushed himself up and put his mouth against one hardened nipple, encircling the other with his fingers. The contact snapped his control, and everything he had been holding back rushed forward.

Liz joined him in the deluge. Feelings poured through her like water released from a floodgate, knocking aside the questions that had plagued her earlier in the evening. For one glorious, perfectly harmonious moment, she had no doubts about the very rightness of being with Nathan.

If I can just hold on to this moment.

The wish stayed with her, repeating itself again and again while they floated down from the heights of passion. The harmony lingered while Nathan picked up every scrap of scattered paper, and they turned sorting those papers into a game of kiss and tease and laughter.

''Now will you tell me what was bothering you earlier?'' he asked when they had settled in bed for the second time.

Liz snuggled close to him. In his arms and sated by his loving, the anxieties and doubts of today seemed unreal. So instead of telling him what had really upset her, she blamed her preoccupation on the problems of the tenants in Claxton Summerfield's apartment buildings. Nathan listened, murmuring sympathetically in all the right places. Warmed by his concern, she fell into a peaceful sleep.

But could she really forget all her doubts? Liz awoke with that question the next morning. She had always prided herself on being a levelheaded woman. Sensations had never ruled her life. She had never regarded sex as the most important ingredient in a relationship. Yet when Nathan looked at her in that devouring way of his, she forgot that those eyes grew equally hungry when he talked business or greeted a prospective client.

His ambition and herself. They both made strong claims on Nathan. But which was the stronger? And which would win if put to the test? She wasn't sure she wanted to know.

Days passed. A week. Then almost two. Liz could always forget her doubts when she was in Nathan's arms, when he was making her laugh or being his charmingly irreverent self. But there were other moments when doubts were all she had. She was feeling those doubts intensely on a mid-February evening after a meeting of Aunt Eugenia's charity auction committee.

Like an accomplished delegator, Eugenia had paid a customary brief visit, staying only long enough to see that all plans were being carried out. Eugenia left, and in the way of most such gatherings, the meeting became decidedly social. Committee members lingered, drinking coffee and talking in the conference room of the real-estate development firm where tonight's meeting had been held. Nathan's attention was centered on a beautiful blond architect.

Beautiful, blond and a good business prospect. Watching them together made Liz uneasy.

It's nothing, she thought. *I'm just feeling a squeeze from the green-eyed jealousy monster.*

Silently she recited all the reasons why she shouldn't be jealous. She had come to this meeting with Nathan. She would leave with him. She would sleep beside him tonight. Just this morning he had made love to her in such a thorough, distracting way she had been late for a court appearance.

And the blonde doesn't know what it's like to make love with Nathan Hollister, she assured herself. Then she narrowed her eyes as the woman laughed and put her hand on Nathan's arm. He didn't move away, and Liz took a deep swallow from the cup of coffee she'd been nursing for the last half hour.

"He's into the spirit of things, isn't he?"

The amused comment startled Liz, and she turned to find Cassandra sitting down beside her at the conference table.

Cassandra wasn't officially on the auction committee, but she had come to all the meetings. She had surprised everyone by staying in Nashville after Christmas, and she seemed to be making good on her vow to start a theater arts program for disadvantaged youths. She had already cajoled a donation from her father, found a building and started soliciting money from other sources.

"Maybe I should talk Nathan into helping me with my school," she continued, nodding toward the corner where he and the blonde stood. "He seems to take to charity work with enthusiasm."

Liz decided to ignore her friend's mocking tone. "Nathan's very happy to be working on the auction," she murmured.

Cassandra chuckled. "That was lame, Liz, 'specially for such a hotshot attorney."

"I don't know what you're talking about."

"I've known you all my life, and I can tell when you're jealous."

"That's absurd—"

Another burst of laughter sounded from Nathan and his companion, and Cassandra slanted another look at them. "Want me to go engage her in conversation? I could ask her who spray-paints her hair."

"Cassandra, please," Liz murmured. "I'm sure she and Nathan are talking business. He'd like to represent this firm. They're doing very well, and she's a partner. Her father's in charge."

"How lucky for Nathan that he's on this little old committee with her."

Liz glanced sharply at her friend. "What do you mean by that?"

"Just that this seems to have been a *valuable* experience for Nathan." Cassandra made a great show of studying her crimson-painted nails. "Last time I counted, he'd already made clients out of several other members."

Liz shrugged, determined to act unconcerned. "If it bothers you, maybe you shouldn't count."

"You're the one I would expect to be bothered."

"There's no reason why a person can't combine business with a little charity work."

"Or a *little* charity with a lot of business."

"Okay, Cassandra," Liz said, giving into her irritation. "What is the point of this? I know you don't like Nathan—"

"I never said that."

"But you criticize him every chance you get."

Sighing, Cassandra pushed a strand of curly dark hair behind her ear. "I'm sorry," she murmured, and raised genuinely contrite eyes to Liz. "I really don't dislike him, and I can see how much you care for him."

Liz glanced down at the legal pad in front of her. "Oh, can you?"

"You've always been transparent, Liz. You're crazy about the man."

To her consternation, a blush spread across Liz's cheeks. "He's pretty special," she admitted. "Maybe that's why I was sitting here getting jealous over someone who means absolutely nothing to him."

"Nothing but business," Cassandra murmured. Her eyebrows drew together in a frown. "Maybe it's how much his business means to him that you really have to worry about."

Liz swallowed hard. Darn Cassandra anyway, for painting the fears Liz wanted to hide in giant, impossible-to-ignore letters.

"I'm not worried," she lied.

Cassandra's expression was skeptical, but she said nothing more. Maggie joined them, Nathan finally left the architect's side, and the conversation moved to Cassandra's school.

Yet Liz couldn't get rid of her uneasiness. Especially when she caught the glance the blond architect sent Nathan's way when he said goodbye. His own eyes were cool, his handshake businesslike. But Liz was left to wonder. . . .

Just how far would he go in the name of ambition?

Thank goodness the next few days were too filled with activity to leave her much time for pondering that disquieting thought. She had a difficult case, a vagrant accused of a string of downtown holdups he said he hadn't committed. The evidence said otherwise, and she fought an uphill battle. Her losing verdict came in late Thursday afternoon. Disgruntled, Liz got to the office just as the receptionist was leaving for the day.

"Cheryl Lockhart called about three times," the woman said. "She sounded upset. Since she doesn't have a phone, she said she'd call you back."

"What a great way to end the day," Liz muttered, knowing she had to disappoint Cheryl. Yesterday she had received a reply to the letter she had sent Claxton Summerfield. The letter was actually from his representative, a man named Eldon Rogers, and in it the Summerfield Properties Corporation refused to buy materials for all but the most minor of the improvements to his apartment buildings. Liz hadn't had time to let the tenants know, and she was toying with another, more direct approach to the problem.

She had just sat down at her desk when the phone rang. It was Cheryl.

"Mr. Summerfield didn't like that letter," the woman said without preamble.

"I know," Liz replied, searching for the man's letter on her desk.

"He sent a man, one of his top men, around here to talk to me."

Liz sat up, startled. "What?"

"You don't need to bother him anymore," Cheryl added. "It'll just cause more problems."

"Cheryl, I told you he can't throw you out of your home. You're not behind on the rent, are you?"

"Yes, but that's not what I'm worried about. The doctor says Marissa might need surgery on her arm."

"And Summerfield promised to pay for that."

"Promises get broken."

Liz sighed in frustration. "Cheryl, his company put that promise in writing."

"But if he wanted to, he could break it, and I couldn't fight him."

"Yes, you could. I would help."

"No," the woman murmured. "No, I don't need your help."

Rubbing at the ache in her temples, Liz tried to think of something to reassure Cheryl. Something wasn't right. Cheryl didn't sound like herself. "Just what did Summerfield's representative say to you? Did he threaten you?"

"No...not exactly."

"Then why are you acting so frightened?"

The woman's voice rose. "Listen, Miss Patterson, I appreciate what you tried to do for us. But maybe that man is right. Maybe where we live is all we can expect for the amount of rent we pay."

"And what about everyone else? Do they all want me to drop it?"

Cheryl hesitated. "I guess you'll have to ask them. But if they do anything else, I'm going to be blamed."

"That's ridiculous, and giving up doesn't sound like you."

Cheryl gave a short, mirthless laugh. "Yeah, well, maybe I'm just getting smart about this world. Roy always told me I would someday."

"But, Cheryl—"

"I got no money," the woman interrupted harshly. "I got three kids, a lousy job and an even lousier man, and if I have to pay a bunch of doctor's bills, I'm in deeper than ever. Maybe that don't mean anything to you—"

"Of course it does."

"Sure." The disbelief came through loud and clear in that one word. "I'm thinkin' about just sending my kids to my parents for a while. They got it tough, too, but I just don't know if I can make it on my own much longer."

Hearing this proud, resourceful woman sound so defeated was more than Liz could bear. "Oh, Cheryl, please let me help—"

"No," she said slowly. "No, thank you, ma'am."

"Cheryl—"

She hung up, and Liz stared at the receiver, feeling as if she'd been slapped. How long she sat there, she couldn't say. But the offices were empty and dark when she looked up and saw Nathan standing in the doorway.

"Something wrong?" he asked, flipping the light switch.

Blinking against the sudden glare, Liz nodded, but she didn't say anything. She didn't even notice that Nathan came around the desk. All she could hear was

Cheryl's quiet, faintly accusing voice telling her to butt out.

"Liz?" She glanced up into Nathan's concerned hazel eyes. He was leaning against the desk, frowning. "What's wrong?"

"Everything, I guess," she murmured.

"Tell me about it." He drew her to her feet and into his arms.

How nice it was to lean on him, to settle her head against his shoulder and let him stroke her hair while she poured out all the details of her long, rotten day. When she got to Cheryl Lockhart's call, she grew angry. "I'd like to know exactly what that Summerfield had his man say to her. Cheryl told me she didn't need my help, but—"

"Oh, Liz," Nathan murmured. "When are you going to realize not everyone wants your help?"

It was the wrong thing to say. He knew that the moment the words left his mouth, and he steeled himself for the coming explosion. Liz stiffened in his arms. Her eyes were flashing when she drew away.

"I'm not the issue here. That man sent someone to intimidate a helpless woman."

"And he shouldn't have," Nathan agreed. "But that doesn't mean it's your problem."

"So you think I should drop it?"

He hesitated, then nodded. "Let it cool off."

"Until someone gets hurt or maybe killed?"

"If you think it's that serious, call whoever inspects buildings."

Liz made a disgusted sound. "Summerfield probably pays them off."

"Well, then you could fight them."

"Shouldn't I?"

Mentally counting to ten, Nathan took a deep breath. "Liz, I don't think we should get into an argument about something we already know we disagree on."

Her eyes very cool, she backed away from him. "No, we should talk about it. Because what I do means a great deal to me—"

"What you do?" he repeated. "How does this Summerfield deal have anything to do with your job?"

"It started out as a case."

"Yes, *started out*." Folding his arms, Nathan perched on the edge of the desk. He didn't want to argue with Liz, but, dammit, this was for her own good. "What *started out* as a case quickly became a cause. That happens all the time to you."

She tossed her head. "Does something about that offend you?"

"No," he muttered, straightening. "But it hurts me to see you so torn up about the lives of people you barely know."

"So I should be more like you—write a check and consider my conscience clear?"

"Oh, God." He thrust his hands into his pockets to keep from shaking her. "Sometimes you can be the most smug, sanctimonious—"

"And you can be the coldest, most apathetic—"

"Great," he cut in, his voice rising. "Now we can hear all about my shortcomings in generosity. Well, let me tell you something, Liz, everyone can't play Lady Bountiful like you do."

"It's a choice *some* people make."

"And it's easy to decide what other people should do when you've got all the options in the world."

"Options?"

"Yeah, when you've been given everything a person could possibly want, you can spread the bounty and stand in judgment of those who can't be quite so generous with their time or their energy or their money."

She laughed. "Oh, dear me, and poor little Nathan has been so deprived."

That made him so angry, he did grasp her by the shoulders. "Everything I have I've worked for, Liz."

"And I don't work?" she asked, twisting out of his grasp.

"I didn't say that. I said you didn't have to *worry* about working. I do, and you know it."

"And I guess success has to mean everything in the world to you, too, doesn't it?" Liz challenged.

A muscle jumped in his cheek as he stepped forward. "Not everything, Liz."

Her eyes filled with tears. "I don't know if that's really true, Nathan. I don't think you know it, either."

The accusation caught him like a punch to the gut. It was direct. It cut right through all the little games he had been playing with himself over the last month. He could stop deluding himself. For it wasn't enough to share just moments with this woman, to commit himself halfway, to think a day-to-day sort of relationship would work. She wanted it all. Dammit, she deserved it all.

And he wasn't sure if he had that much to give.

"You're right," he whispered. "Absolutely right, Liz. I don't know how my priorities stand, and until I do, maybe I should just leave you alone."

He left, his footsteps sounding hollow in the empty offices. It wasn't until she heard the outer door shut that Liz found enough air in her lungs to try to call him back.

But by then it was too late.

Eight

By two o'clock that morning Nathan knew he had made a mistake.

At the same time he realized he was in love with Liz.

He loved her. The admission made his head ache and dulled the bite of the bourbon he was drinking. He took another gulp, anyway, and drew in a deep breath as it burned its way down his throat. Good Lord, how had this happened?

Love wasn't an emotion he knew much about. He supposed he loved his grandparents. Supposed? That was lame. He could imagine Liz's reaction if he said he *supposed* he loved his family. She just loved—with no qualifications—and received love in return. It had never been so easy for him.

Oh, his grandparents loved him in their own vague, self-involved way. They depended on him, wanted to see him. They seemed to care if he was happy, and as he had once told Liz, they were all he had of family. That made some sort of bond. But Nathan had always known he came second to his grandfather's many romantic escapades and his grandmother's friends and bridge partners. As for his father, Nathan had known exactly where he had stood with him—he was a reminder of a broken heart. No matter what Nathan did, he couldn't make his father love him.

But he had tried. Being the best had mattered more than anything to his father, so Nathan had been the best. The smartest student. The top athlete. The college graduate with the most job offers. The young executive with the biggest salary and the best perks. But his father had died without ever telling Nathan that he approved, that he was proud or that he cared. By that time, however, striving for perfection and success was second nature to Nathan. It was all he knew.

And it wasn't good enough for Liz.

Muttering a curse, he tossed down the rest of his drink and stood. This was just his luck. When there were so many women who shared his outlook on life, women who had similar goals and aspirations, he had to pick someone who didn't give a damn about career advancement or five-year plans for personal success. Liz would probably think more of him if he gave away all his possessions and moved to South Africa to battle apartheid.

"This is so stupid," he told his silent apartment. He and Liz were throwing something good away because she thought his ambition was selfish. But what did his ambitions have to do with what they had together? They had passion, and they had laughter. And he was in love with her. They were two intelligent, mature adults, and surely they had enough in common to work through a few philosophical and ideological differences. They should just agree to disagree about certain subjects.

As for his priorities...that was nonsense, too, and he should have realized it before getting angry and leaving her with the wrong impression tonight. His career and his ambitions had nothing to do with how he felt about Liz. The two things should never have become a joint issue. For why would they ever be in conflict? He couldn't imagine a scenario where he would have to choose between loving Liz and attaining a goal.

Keeping that thought firmly in mind, he pulled on his jacket and headed for Liz's apartment. He cautioned himself to be calm and reasonable and logical.

She came to the door on the third ring of the doorbell, and she didn't look as if she'd been asleep. In fact, her eyelashes were suspiciously damp, her nose was red, and she had the pale, wrung-out look of someone who had been crying.

Her fragile, exhausted look sent every calm, reasoned bit of logic fleeing from Nathan's brain. What he said came straight from his heart. "I love you."

Liz took a step backward. "What?"

"I love you," Nathan repeated, sounding angry. "Now can I come in?"

Like a sleepwalker, she moved aside. Then they faced each other across her living room. Nathan looked defiant, the most un-loverlike stance Liz could possibly imagine.

"I love you," he said for the third time.

His repetition began to make her angry. Who was he trying to convince, himself or her? "You don't sound as if you're happy about it."

He shifted from foot to foot. "I didn't intend to tell you this way."

"You didn't intend to love me at all, did you?"

"That's not..." He faltered, obviously thinking better of the denial he had been ready to utter. "You're right," he admitted after a pause. "Loving you wasn't what I planned at all."

"Then why do you?"

He frowned. "That's a strange question."

"Well, isn't everything about your life some grand, perfectly synchronized scheme? Why is there suddenly room for me in it?"

Nathan bowed his head for a moment. He guessed he deserved that remark. Up until now he had moved from one part of his life to the next like a master chess player navigating a board. Liz was his first detour. He wanted to make sure they both didn't get lost.

He looked back at her, gathering all his courage. "Does it really matter why I love you, Liz? Can't it be enough that I do?"

She said nothing, staring at him with big, hopelessly blue eyes.

He took a step forward. "And don't you love me? Even just a little?"

Tears trembled on her lashes. She wiped at them impatiently as she answered, "You can't love someone just a little bit, Nathan. At least I can't. And I do love you."

The admission, no matter how grudgingly it was given, filled Nathan's heart to bursting. He closed the gap between them, gathering her close just as the first sob broke from her. "You don't sound too happy about it, either."

"I'm not," she choked out, pushing away from him. "I don't want to love you, either. You're not anything like the man I always thought I'd love."

"And who were you saying had their life all planned?" Nathan whispered.

"Oh, darn it," Liz muttered, swiping at the tears on her cheeks. "Why do I have to cry, anyway? I never cry."

With his hand under her chin, he lifted her face. "Is loving me really so awful?" He touched his mouth to hers then—gently, tasting her tears, stilling the faint tremble of her lips. "Does that feel wrong?"

"That isn't the problem," Liz said, shutting her eyes. "When you touch me, I believe everything's going to be fine. And then—"

"Maybe I should just touch you more often," Nathan suggested before capturing her lips again.

Liz broke away. "Don't . . . don't do that."

"But everything else is so unimportant. What else can matter when I feel this way about you?" He placed her hand over his chest. He was warm against the coldness of her hand, and even through his sweater she could feel his heart pounding. "What can come between us when we know how right it can feel?"

His words made sense, especially when followed by the intoxicating movement of his lips against her own. But Liz wasn't going to give in to sensation. Not this time. "I have to know I come first with you," she said. "That's the only way I know how to love, Nathan."

"Of course you come first." He framed her face with his hands. "I love you, Liz. Only you. I've never loved anyone else."

"I'm not worried about other people. Your work—"

"Just stop it," he muttered fiercely, his hands dropping to her shoulders. "Stop trying to invent a problem where none exists. I love you. You love me. That has nothing to do with anything else—not my work, not how I feel about each and every one of your causes."

But how he felt about the things that were important to her had everything to do with who he was and how they would make it together. Liz couldn't understand why he didn't see that.

"Love me, Liz. Just concentrate on that."

"Love isn't always the answer."

"It depends on the question."

"Nathan—"

"Just love me," he repeated. "Please."

He wasn't the kind of man who begged. If anything, he was the complete opposite. She suspected he'd do without basic necessities rather than ask. But he was begging for her love.

"You can't imagine what knowing that you care means to me," he continued. "Sometimes when I come home to you, when you smile at me in that special way of yours . . ." He paused, and though Liz could see he tried to control it, his voice shook when he continued. "Sometimes I can't believe how lucky I am, Liz. I'm lucky because you care what happens to me."

Those simple words told her everything about the lonely heart hiding behind his carefree facade. No one had ever let him know he was really and truly loved. *Damn his family,* she thought. *Don't they know how much they hurt him?*

"I love you, Nathan," she murmured. Her arms stole around him, holding him close. "I do love you. Please don't ever forget that."

He kissed her again, a kiss full of yearning that had nothing to do with sex. He was just one human being who needed the warmth, the caring of another. The kiss deepened, of course. It changed. It became a lover's kiss. Liz didn't think she'd ever be able to kiss Nathan without the heat. Spontaneous combustion, she thought, remembering Cassandra's description. They would always have that fire—even if she kissed him every day for the rest of their lives.

And that was what she wanted—the rest of their lives. Together. But she wasn't confident about getting her wish.

Unlike Nathan, she didn't think their loving each other solved their problems. Her doubts couldn't be erased, no matter how many times they made slow, exquisitely perfect love. No matter how often he repeated the words.

Instead of growing closer, admitting their feelings to each other seemed to send them in the opposite direction. Days passed, and they began to tiptoe around each other. Their spontaneity was gone. Nathan didn't come home with war stories about difficult clients he had pleased or displeased. He didn't tell her about plans he was making for the firm. Liz did her best not to sound like a crusader, even when she was bursting at the seams to share something that had happened. It was as if they were both determined not to give the other a reason to disapprove.

A chasm grew and deepened between them, and Liz found herself waiting for their fragile world to simply split apart.

In the yard at her parents' home, daffodils were pushing toward the bright sunshine as Liz walked to the side door. It was hard to imagine, but it was already the middle of March. In another month her parents would be home from Europe. She looked forward to seeing them, and to introducing them to Nathan.

Nathan. Thinking of him, Liz paused at the flower-bed beside the kitchen porch. Nathan had kissed her here on Christmas Eve, and afterward she had been forced to admit how much he really meant to her. That night she'd had no idea how complicated everything was going to become. Sighing, she stooped down to examine the narrow green shoots, breathing in the smell of damp earth and awakening flowers. When these flowers had finished budding and before her parents came home, she and Nathan might be finished, too.

Last night, for the first time in over a month, he hadn't spent the night with her. She shivered despite the warm spring breeze, remembering the cold, polite way they had dealt with each other.

It had started out as a nice evening. She had won the case of a college student falsely accused of rape. Her defense had been tricky, and the victory had her flying high by the time she met Nathan for dinner. He'd had a great day, too, although as usual he hadn't gone into any details. But they had ordered champagne and celebrated their mutual successes. When had the glow faded? Liz wondered. It was as if after an hour or so of spontaneity, they remembered to be careful with each other, to not say anything that might start a disagreement.

After dinner Nathan had pleaded work at the office. He had said he would be very late and would just go on to his place afterward. Liz had tried to be nonchalant about it, but she had missed him more than she would have ever expected. The bed had seemed big and empty, and she had felt terribly alone. It was perhaps only the first of many such lonely nights.

While she frowned over that thought, Jeannette bustled out of the kitchen. "So, *chérie*, what do you make of the flowers? A sure sign of spring, right?"

"Right," Liz replied, standing.

"And spring should make you happy."

"I am happy."

Jeannette's brown eyes surveyed Liz shrewdly. "Why am I not convinced? Where's that pretty smile?"

Against her will, Liz grinned. Jeannette had always been able to coax her out of the doldrums. "I'll smile all afternoon if you made my favorite brownies for tea."

"I did, but Cassandra has been here for half an hour. So you know the brownies might be gone." Laughing now, Liz followed the older woman into the house.

Eugenia was waiting in the front parlor with Cassandra, who looked like spring personified in a daffodil-yellow dress. The color made Liz long for something lighter than her own green wool suit.

"Where's Maggie?" she asked, taking a seat on the sofa beside Eugenia. "I thought I was late."

"Maggie has a new beau," Eugenia said. "She's helping him redecorate his house, and she said she'd probably be running behind schedule this afternoon."

"A new beau," Liz echoed. She accepted a cup of tea and a brownie and relaxed against the cushions. When had Maggie met someone new? The last few weeks had been devoted to her job, to organizing a tenants' protest at the Summerfield buildings, and to her problems with Nathan. She had seen little of her friends or her aunt. As it was, she had left a stack of work on her desk in order to play hooky and have this early tea with Eugenia. "Do you approve of Maggie's new man, Eugenia?"

Eugenia shrugged, her eyebrows arching delicately. "I haven't had the pleasure of meeting him yet."

"So he wasn't one of your brainstorms," Cassandra observed. "Umm, maybe there's hope for this one."

"We'll see," Eugenia said, fixing the pretty brunette with her gaze. "Speaking of beaux—what happened with that young man who escorted you to the charity auction?"

The long-awaited auction had taken place last Saturday night. They had set a record in attendance and in money raised, but Liz thought the highlight of the evening had been watching Cassandra try to ditch the date Eugenia had arranged for her.

Setting her teacup on the coffee table with a clatter, Cassandra frowned. "Liz, remind me to say no the next time Eugenia tries to fix me up." She shuddered. "I had the worst time of my life Saturday night. It's taken me almost a week to get over the boredom that man caused."

Liz chuckled. "I could have warned you—"

"Horse feathers!" Eugenia was glaring at Cassandra. "You just don't get into the spirit of things, girl. You won't give anyone a chance. If you ask me, you're carrying a torch for someone."

A rare flush colored Cassandra's cheeks. "If I were carrying a torch, and I'm not saying I am, that man you made me go out with would not extinguish the flame."

"Give him a chance," Eugenia said. "Just look at Liz. She didn't like Nathan at first, either. And now they're the perfect couple."

Liz nearly choked on a bite of brownie. Quickly she washed the morsel down with tea, trying to avoid Eugenia's sharpened regard. She was steeling herself for an interrogation when they heard the front door open and close.

Maggie breezed into the room on a cloud of fragrance from the tissue-wrapped bouquet of flowers she carried. Her smile was brighter than the sunshine outside. "Isn't it the most wonderful, perfect day?" she asked by way of greeting.

"I hadn't noticed," Eugenia retorted with unusual asperity. "And what's got you looking like the first blossom of spring?"

"Love," Maggie sighed. "Love and springtime. They're just perfect together." She glanced around in surprise as the other three groaned. "What's wrong with all of you?"

Cassandra rolled her eyes. Eugenia snorted. Liz murmured a quiet, "Don't ask."

Putting the flowers down on an end table, Maggie took the chair beside Cassandra's. "If I had known I was coming to a wake instead of tea party, I would have stayed with Don. He's much better company."

"So his name is Don," Eugenia murmured. "And when are we going to meet this man who's put such a sparkle in your eyes?"

Smiling mysteriously as she poured herself a cup of tea, Maggie's reply was an evasive, "Soon."

Eugenia waited expectantly. "That's all you're going to say about him?"

"For right now." Maggie took a sip of tea. "But I think you can officially take me off your matchmaking list, Eugenia. I believe I'm taken."

"Oh Lordy," Cassandra said, rolling her eyes again. "And that just leaves me. Liz, don't you and Nathan need some of Eugenia's guidance?"

The silence that followed was telling, but try as she might, Liz couldn't think of anything to break it.

"Sorry, Liz." Cassandra got up to steal another brownie from the tea tray. "You know me and my big mouth."

Eugenia was studying Liz with concern. "And what's wrong with you and Nathan?"

Very carefully, Liz placed her teacup on the table. Just as carefully, she arranged the front pleats in her skirt. She started to speak, but to her consternation tears sprang to her eyes. She had become a regular waterworks lately.

"Liz," Eugenia said, touching her arm. "Liz, dear, what's wrong?"

Liz blinked away her tears and managed to force her voice around the giant-sized lump in her throat. "Nathan and I aren't doing too well."

"But you love him."

And how did she know that? Liz gazed at her aunt, amazed as usual by the woman's intuitive powers.

"Don't you know by now that we can't hide anything from her?" Maggie said softly.

"It's one of those things I count on," Cassandra added, without a trace of her usual sarcasm. "I know Eugenia's always going to know what I'm thinkin' before I think it myself."

"None of you are very hard to read." Eugenia gripped Liz's hand with her own. "Especially not my Liz." There was a hint of a tremble in her voice, but she cleared it away quickly. "Now tell me, what has Nathan done?"

"It's nothing he's done. We're just so very different, too different for it to work."

"Explain."

Liz tried, but she found it difficult to put all her doubts and fears into words. Even their differences seemed petty when she laid them out for the others to examine.

Eugenia seemed particularly unimpressed. "Goodness, Liz, you act as if two people have to agree on every little thing. Wherever did you get such a ridiculous notion?"

"But we approach life so differently. Nathan is controlled by his ambition."

"I don't think I understand why you resent his ambition so much," Maggie said, frowning.

"Resent?" Liz had never thought of her feelings as resentment. "That's not—"

"But of course you resent it," Cassandra interrupted. "I knew this would cause problems, Liz. You're just not the kind of person who identifies with people who are driven to succeed. You're too selfless for that." She paused, frowning. "Although come to think of it, you're pretty driven yourself."

Eugenia murmured her agreement.

"What do you mean?" Liz asked.

"Are you any less committed to your job or your causes than Nathan is to his work?" Eugenia didn't even pause for an answer. "Of course you aren't. You're both consumed by what you do. I believe that's part of what makes you right for each other. You're both strong, independent people with your own interests. Any other type would bore you both."

"But there's a difference," Liz insisted. "Nathan can be ruthless when he wants something. He can play any role he needs to in order to make a point or impress someone. He's like a chameleon."

"Isn't that just business?" Cassandra asked.

"Maybe," Liz answered. "But if he can be that way about what he does, why shouldn't I worry that he would be the same in regard to me?"

Maggie leaned forward in her chair, her brown eyes full of concern. "Has he treated you that way, Liz?"

"Well...no, not yet anyway. But I know what comes first with him," Liz rushed to add. "And it's not me. No matter what he says to the contrary, I know what I care about will always come second to him. First priority goes to what he wants and what serves him best."

"So you're saying Nathan should only care about those things that matter to you?" Eugenia murmured.

Put that way, Liz thought she sounded as selfish as she had accused Nathan of being. "That's not it, not completely." Frustrated, she smoothed an errant strand of hair back into her neat chignon and lapsed into silence. "I guess I've explained this badly."

"No, I think I understand." Her expression grave, Maggie came and perched on the arm of the sofa where Liz sat. "You think if Nathan were given the choice between pleasing you and an opportunity to advance himself, he would choose the opportunity."

"I know he would."

"And what about you?" Eugenia's voice held an accusing note. "Would you give up something you cared about for Nathan?"

"Of course."

Her aunt's still-brilliant blue eyes searched Liz's face. "You're quick to say what you would do now. But when and if you were given the choice, it might be harder to decide."

"Wait a minute," Cassandra cut in. "It sounds to me as if you're all saying that for love to succeed, someone has to give something up. What happened to equality, to being true to yourself?''

Eugenia's laughter spilled out. ''I believe in all those fine notions, Cassandra, dear. But I also know something about relationships. They don't work without compromise.''

''And I'm the one who should make the concessions, right?'' Liz muttered.

''No,'' Eugenia replied carefully. ''But I do think you should give Nathan the benefit of the doubt before you dismiss him from your life. He just might surprise you.''

Maggie stood and picked up the flowers she had tossed on the table. Her gaze was thoughtful as she touched the colorful spring blossoms. ''Liz, maybe the problem is that you just don't trust Nathan the way you should.''

Sighing, Liz sat up and poured herself some more tea. ''Where does trust come from?''

''Time,'' Eugenia said with a pause. ''Take the time to know each other and then be patient.''

''Good heavens!'' Cassandra literally jumped from her chair and crossed the room to the front window in a swirl of yellow skirts. She thrust the curtains to the side in an impatient gesture. ''I'm certainly glad I don't have any of these romantic problems.''

Liz saw Maggie and Eugenia exchange a conspiratorial smile. She wasn't so consumed by her own problems that she couldn't wonder what they were plotting. Poor Cassandra, she thought. For if Maggie and Eugenia were hatching a matchmaking scheme and it involved the person Liz thought it might, Cassandra might soon be as miserable as Liz was now.

''I'm going to put these in water,'' Maggie said, waving her flowers before she left the room.

Swallowing the last of her tea, Liz glanced at her watch. She put her cup down and stood. "Sorry, but I've got to run. I've got a late meeting."

"Oh, that's no problem." Cassandra turned from the window and teased, "Just take up all our time with your problems and then dash off."

"Send me a bill." Laughing, Liz bent to press a kiss to her aunt's cheek. "Thanks," she whispered.

Eugenia touched her hair. "It can work out, Liz, but only if you want it to."

"I know," Liz agreed, though in reality she didn't know it at all. Calling her goodbyes to the others, she hurried through the house and out to her car. She would think about what Eugenia had said later. First, she had to meet the members of the tenants' association at Summerfield's office. What they were planning to do should keep her mind off of Nathan for several hours, at least.

It was funny how some people came to mean a great deal to you in a short time, Liz thought as she navigated through the heavy afternoon traffic. It was that way for her with these tenants. Though Cheryl Lockhart had indeed taken her children and moved back to her parents' farm, there were others in the buildings who wanted to fight for the needed improvements. Summerfield had shot down all their suggestions, and as he'd done with Cheryl, he had sent a representative out to try to intimidate the other tenants. Remembering Eldon Rogers, the blustering spokesman Summerfield had sent out to do his dirty work, Liz's lips twisted. Obviously, Summerfield was one of those people who hid behind a screen of employees. He'd never had the gumption to even answer any of her letters himself.

Well, his scare tactics hadn't worked. If anything, they'd had the opposite effect. The tenants were willing to fight, and now it was time to get serious. In Liz's trunk was a stack of placards. She smiled, thinking of what Summerfield would do when the tenants began parading those signs in front of his office just as the evening rush hour started. Liz had tipped off the local media. Hopefully the attention would shame the man into living up to his obligations.

Nathan tried for the third time in as many minutes to concentrate on a press release his assistant had put on his desk this morning. It was now almost four, and this had to go out in today's mail. He tried yet again, failed and finally scrawled his approving initials across the bottom of the page. He called his assistant in and told her she'd done a great job.

"At least I hope you did," he murmured as the door closed behind the woman. He rubbed at the ache in his temples and twisted his chair around to face the window.

His preoccupation had started yesterday with an unexpected and disconcerting phone call. It had continued today after a breakfast meeting. Because of that meeting, he had a big decision to make. On the up side, his business would benefit—to put it mildly. On the down side, his relationship with Liz might have just started its final collision course with disaster.

He settled back in his chair, weighing his options. Taking this opportunity would improve his cash flow, but more importantly, the opportunity would be a springboard to bigger things, the sort of challenges and recognition he craved. He could wait forever to be handed this kind of chance again. Without it, he was just one more public relations firm with a modest client list and a few minor success stories. And to Nathan, being mediocre was the same as failure.

On the other hand if he took his chance, Liz might never forgive him. Things between them were strained enough, as it was. This would only make it worse.

Damn, but here was the situation he had never expected to happen—his work in direct conflict with Liz's.

Arm propped on the arm of his chair, Nathan tapped a finger against his mouth while he sightlessly studied the downtown Nashville skyline. His head was telling him to do one thing, his heart another. But surely there was a way to do both and to keep everyone happy.

He remained where he was, thinking, for quite a while. An idea had just occurred to him when the buzz of the phone cut through the silence.

Nathan answered absentmindedly, but he sat up, instantly alert, when he heard the voice on the other end.

"Hollister, this is Claxton Summerfield, and I'd like you to get over to my office this minute. I've got people over here picketing me, and one of the television stations just pulled up. This kind of publicity won't do my candidacy any good. I know you said you needed a day or two to think over our association, but I need you now."

This has to be Liz's work, Nathan thought, feeling the muscle in his cheek begin to jump.

"Hollister?"

"Yes, sir."

"What's it gonna be?"

Nathan hesitated. He supposed he now understood why they said the course of a life could turn on the decisions made in a single moment.

"Hollister?"

Remembering the idea he'd had before the phone rang, Nathan drew a breath and took the plunge. "Okay. I'll be right over."

Nine

It's perfect, Liz thought, absolutely perfect.

Grinning, she crossed her arms and leaned against the marbled exterior wall of the building where Summerfield Properties Corporation's offices were housed. In front of her, twenty-odd tenants marched in orderly fashion, hoisting their brightly lettered placards.

Almost equally divided between men and women, the picketers included almost everyone in the tenants' association who wasn't working at this time of day. Liz had warned them to look their best and not to appear as if this were just a lark. They had complied, and she was proud of the way they were carrying this off.

Sign-waving picket lines weren't the norm in downtown Nashville. Passing cars were slowing to see what the commotion was, and pedestrians were stopping to ask questions. One of the local television stations had just departed. The female reporter had interviewed the tenant association president. He had presented the group's grievances in a clear, concise manner, just the way Liz had coached him. She hadn't had to say a word.

How can Summerfield ignore this? Liz thought.

She was allowing herself just a touch of smugness when she saw Nathan step through the picket line. When he saw her, he looked grim. Liz straightened away from the wall as he came toward her. He came nearer and paused, not saying a word, his face set in troubled lines.

"Nathan?" Liz finally said. "What are you doing here?"

"I . . ." He hesitated, cleared his throat and started again. "Liz, there's something . . ."

"Hollister!"

They both turned as his name was called. A portly, graying man that Liz recognized as Eldon Rogers, Summerfield's pontificating representative, was hurrying down the sidewalk from the entrance. Now how did Rogers know Nathan? Something Liz vaguely recognized as dread began to churn in her stomach.

The man puffed to a stop beside them. "Mr. Summerfield's just inside, waiting for you, Hollister."

Summerfield was waiting for Nathan. It took a minute for the words to sink in, but when they did Liz felt the blood drain from her face. "Nathan?" she whispered, looking at him, waiting for him to tell her this wasn't what it appeared to be.

But his guilt-filled eyes only told her everything she didn't want to know. "I was trying to tell you—"

"Oh, do you and Miss Patterson know each other?" Rogers asked, his shrewd glance going from one to the other.

"Yes, we know each other." Nathan's gaze didn't waver from Liz's. "And if you'll give us a minute—"

"But she's the reason these people are here."

"I said give us a minute," Nathan bit out, glancing at the man in irritation.

"Summerfield—"

"—can wait," Nathan snapped, his expression so ferocious that Rogers retreated without further discussion.

"Goodness," Liz choked out. "You're being awfully cavalier with a client, aren't you?"

"I only just agreed to work with Summerfield, Liz."

She nodded toward the picket line. "He probably only just decided he needed someone to watch out for his public image."

"He's going to run for the Senate," Nathan said. "That's why he hired me. I didn't know you were going to do this."

With a bitter laugh, she tossed her head. "Well isn't that a pity? If we'd been exchanging any pillow talk about this, you could have warned him about this. My, wouldn't that have scored some points for you."

Nathan's voice was deadly calm. "You know I wouldn't have done that."

"Do I?"

"Liz—"

"Why?" she cut in. "Why are you doing this, Nathan? You were bound to know how I would feel about it."

"But I think I can help."

"Help?" Turning her eyes toward the sky, Liz fought to keep her voice under control. "And how are you going to help, Nathan? What kind of slick lies are you going to come up with to make Summerfield look like a saint?''

"Liz, please," he murmured, trying to take her arm.

She jerked away. "Leave me alone, Nathan. I don't want to hear any of your lies, either." Turning on her heel, she hurried down the sidewalk. She was afraid if she stayed here any longer, she'd be physically ill.

Nathan caught up with her, his long stride keeping him easily beside her. "Liz, I want to talk about this. I need to explain."

She didn't even look at him. "You don't have to explain. I've got you all figured out. The terrible thing is that I've understood you from the very beginning, and I let myself be fooled into thinking I might be wrong."

Quickening her pace until she was almost running, Liz wove in and out of a group of office workers who were flooding out of a nearby building. The crowd separated her from Nathan. She heard him call her name, but she didn't look back.

Liz's apartment had never felt so small.

Still in the green suit she'd worn all day, she sprawled on the couch, head aching, staring at the ceiling, listening to the voices of everyone who called and left messages on her answering machine.

Nathan called. Once. Twice. He said there were things she didn't understand, that they needed to talk, that he was going to persuade Summerfield to do something about the tenants' grievances. She just thanked God he didn't say he loved her. Liz was very afraid she would have thrown the telephone up against the wall if he had, and she hoped he didn't show up on her doorstep. She'd lose control if he did.

The president of the tenants' association called, too. Summerfield wanted a meeting tomorrow; did she think that was okay? Remembering her obligations, Liz gathered enough energy to sit up and pick up on the call. Sure, she told him, it was fine if they met with Summerfield, and if he didn't come up with any acceptable offers they'd go back on the picket line.

With the phone still in her lap, she replaced the receiver in its cradle, already dreading the meeting. Nathan would probably be there, decked out in a three-piece suit with briefcase in hand, part of Summerfield's team. She rested her head on the back of the sofa. Was one client really worth the loss of her respect for him?

The answer was a simple yes. Summerfield was running for the Senate. The big time, as Nathan referred to it. God, he must have felt as if he died and went to heaven when Summerfield hired him. This was Nathan's chance, the reason he had gone into business for himself. He would probably direct a landslide victory campaign. Then the sky would be the limit.

He had been given the choice she only theorized about this afternoon with Eugenia and her friends. And he had chosen the opportunity to advance, just as Liz had known he would.

"And I hope it makes him happy," she whispered, squeezing her eyes shut against the tears that threatened. After tonight she promised herself she was never going to cry again, not over a man, anyway.

The phone rang again, and without thinking Liz answered before her machine could pick up. The man on the other end identified himself as Eldon Rogers.

Liz didn't give him a chance to say more than his name. "I understand there's going to be a meeting tomorrow afternoon. I'm sure whatever you want to say can be said then.''

''But I thought we might save everyone the trouble of a meeting.''

''I assure you it will be no trouble,'' Liz replied. ''I've been looking forward to meeting Claxton Summerfield face-to-face. He is going to be there, isn't he?''

''Of course he plans to,'' Rogers said smoothly. ''But I thought if you and I could work something out—''

''I believe we tried that.''

''But that was before I knew you, Miss Patterson.''

She paused, frowning. ''I don't believe we know each other now.''

''Maybe I should say that I understand you now,'' the man continued.

The pounding in Liz's head began to beat in double-time. ''Mr. Rogers, I really have nothing to say to you at this time. Now if—''

''Have you talked with your boyfriend?''

She gripped the smooth plastic of the receiver hard. ''My what?''

''Nathan Hollister. He is your boyfriend, isn't he?''

''That's none of your business.''

''But I disagree,'' Rogers said in a voice that dripped oily, false concern. ''Hollister is working for us—''

''For your boss,'' Liz interrupted.

''Whatever. The point is that Hollister's relationship with you would seem to be in conflict with his work for us.''

''That won't be a problem,'' Liz said dryly. ''Not any more.''

''I could see this afternoon that you'd had a lovers' spat, but—''

"Let me repeat myself," she said sharply. "Mr. Hollister's involvement with me, though it is none of your business, shouldn't present any problems for you."

"But I can't be sure of that, now can I?"

Liz's irritation began to turn to anger. "I have no reason to lie to you."

"Of course you don't," the man soothed. "But if we could work something out with the tenants now, something acceptable, then no one would ever question Hollister's loyalties. His association with Summerfield would never be in jeopardy because of you. I'm sure you wouldn't want that."

As if he had cocked the trigger of a gun, Rogers' words clicked in Liz's brain. Now she knew his game. She definitely understood why he had been able to intimidate Cheryl Lockhart. Full-blown fury crackled through her, making her voice shake. "You're saying that if the tenants give in, Nathan continues to work for Summerfield. But if not, he doesn't. Right?"

"Your words, Miss Patterson. Not mine," he sidestepped expertly. "And the tenants wouldn't have to give in on all points. We could—"

"Forget it," Liz said bluntly. "Forget your threats. Forget it all. And don't call me back." She slammed the phone down.

"That slime." She racked her brain, trying to think of all the colorful, irreverent curses she had ever heard. None of them could begin to describe this contemptible jerk. Oh, but Nathan had gotten himself mixed up with a wonderful group of people. She wondered what he would do if he knew what Rogers had just threatened. Maybe if he knew, he wouldn't be so eager to help Summerfield get elected. Ambitious though Nathan was, Liz didn't think he'd sit still for what Rogers had just tried.

At least she hoped he wouldn't.

There was only one way to find out. She'd tell him. She dialed his home number. His machine came on, and Liz left a message, expecting at any moment for Nathan to break in when he heard her voice. When he didn't, she glanced at her watch. It wasn't very late. He was probably still at his office. She got her purse and left before she could change her mind.

The last person Nathan was expecting to knock at his office door was Liz. If she hadn't already seen him through the windows of the glassed-in reception area, he wasn't sure he would have let her in. For he could see by the stubborn set of her chin that she was still angry. Obviously she hadn't come to tell him she understood what he was doing.

Silently he unlocked the door and opened it for her to pass. "Are you okay?" he asked, knowing instantly how inane the question was.

"Oh, I'm just great," she replied in a falsely bright voice. "This has been a terrific day."

Discouraged by her sarcasm, Nathan ruffled a hand through his hair. It was nearly impossible to reason with Liz when she was like this. He hated to even attempt it. But he had to. "I'd like to explain."

"You don't have to. I understand that this was an opportunity you couldn't let pass."

Some of the tension went out of his neck. Maybe she did understand somewhat. "Why don't we go sit down in my office and talk this over?"

"I think I'd rather stay here."

"Okay, then have a seat."

"I'll stand, thank you."

He frowned at her formal tone. "Liz, come on, don't act as if I committed a crime. I've got Summerfield talked into a compromise with the tenants. It's in his own best interest, of course. In fact, he's eager—"

"—to shaft them, I bet."

"Liz, please."

"I don't want to hear about your compromises." She made a dismissive motion with her hand. "But I think you need to know what Summerfield just did." Quickly, not pausing to give him a chance to interrupt, she told him about Rogers' call and his thinly veiled threats.

The information confirmed some suspicions Nathan had about Rogers. *What a weasel the man was.* Aloud, he said, "I figured he'd do something like this."

Liz fell back a step. "You figured?"

"There's something about that man—"

"And I guess you thought I'd give in to his threats in order to save your big opportunity, didn't you?"

He glanced up. She wasn't listening to him. "Liz—"

"I can't believe you. You expected the man to try and use you to get to me? And that didn't bother you?"

"Liz, you're not being fair."

"Fair!" Her voice rose, and Nathan saw her struggle to get it under control. "Tell me this," she whispered, stepping closer to him. "Is Summerfield a fair man? He's tried using you—"

"It was Rogers who called."

Her mouth twisted into a bitter imitation of a smile. "Oh, and that makes it okay, doesn't it? You're forgetting that Rogers is only Summerfield's puppet. He's the same one Summerfield sent out to intimidate Cheryl Lockhart. Are you trying to say Summerfield didn't know anything about it?"

"That's what confuses me," Nathan replied. "Because the Claxton Summerfield I've dealt with so far doesn't seem like the kind of man who would do any of this. The whole situation seems to have him bewildered."

Liz sucked in her breath. "This is how you justify doing what you do, isn't it? You convince yourself that the people you work for are always right. You close your eyes to their faults. That's how you can lie about them, because you believe the lies."

It hurt to hear what she thought him capable of. More than that, however, it made him furious. Anger crackled through Nathan, sending a hot flush to his face. For such a supposedly fair-minded, liberal person—an attorney, no less—she could close her mind to the facts when it suited her personal purposes. "Tell me something," he demanded. "Have you believed in the innocence of every person you ever defended in court?"

The question took Liz by surprise, and she faltered. "That's differ..." she began, but then stopped. How many times had she thought she was different, her purposes nobler than Nathan's? That reasoning had never seemed trite until now.

Nathan seized upon her hesitation and hammered the point home. "It's always *different* when it's something you want, isn't it, Liz?"

That was exactly what Eugenia had told her that afternoon. Liz's righteous indignation began to crumble.

Nathan crossed the reception area and opened the door to his office. "Tell you what," he said, his voice cold and tight and full of hurt. "Why don't you go home? And maybe tomorrow, or whenever you decide you can listen to me without making judgments and assumptions, maybe then we'll talk this through. Until then, I don't have anything else to say to you.''

"Nathan—"

He didn't wait to see if she left. Instead he slammed his office door so hard the glass rattled in the reception area's windows.

Liz took a step toward the door. Then backed away. It had all gone so wrong, so completely, horribly wrong, and she was beginning to see part of the fault was hers. She couldn't face Nathan again until she sorted that out in her mind.

Nathan felt like punching holes in walls or tossing chairs through the windows. Liz certainly had some kind of power over him. She could make him gut-twisting mad just as quickly as she filled him with desire. He had never imagined that anyone could control him that way.

This was all a mistake. A stupid, foolish mistake. If he had it all to do again, he would turn Claxton Summerfield down on the first phone call.

Nathan knew Liz would never believe his motives had been anything but selfish. But he had truly believed he could convince Summerfield to do something about those apartment buildings. After all, a slum lord had little chance of making it to the Senate, but the cleanup of an unsafe building could be turned to a candidate's advantage. When Summerfield had called this afternoon, Nathan had been envisioning how the man could make himself look like a hero by doing exactly what Liz and his tenants wanted. The motives might not be pure, but the result would be the same. Nathan was sure Liz wouldn't see it that way.

Suddenly exhausted, he sat down at his desk and looked over the press releases he had been drafting when

Liz had shown up. Part of his plan was working. Summerfield *was* going to agree to most of the tenants' demands. Hopefully the details would be ironed out at tomorrow's meeting, and Nathan would release the news to the press. Summerfield would look like a good guy who had made a mistake and was rectifying it.

The funny thing was, he hadn't been all that concerned about his image. True, he had to have been a little worried. Otherwise he wouldn't have called Nathan. But he had seemed most interested in just doing the right thing. It had been Eldon Rogers who had huffed and puffed around, worrying about how all this was going to look.

Tapping his pen against the edge of the desk, Nathan thought back over this afternoon's meeting. Rogers knew Summerfield was going to help the tenants. So why had the man thought it necessary to try to threaten Liz into dropping the matter? It was almost as if Rogers didn't want Liz and Summerfield to get together, to talk. It made it seem as if Rogers had something to hide.

Following his gut instinct, Nathan pulled a business card from his file, picked up the phone and punched in a number.

When the man he wanted was on the line, he identified himself and said, "We need to talk." He paused for the reply. "Why? Because I need some answers before we go any further."

The clear night sky held only questions for Liz. Every high, twinkling star seemed to be asking her why she had been so stupid.

Since leaving Nathan's office, she had driven at least once around the city. Going home was impossible.

Every corner of her apartment would echo some laughter they had shared. Her bed would only remind her of the passion he had shown her. She had been so dumb. So self-righteously stupid and thoughtless. Every bit as guilty of tunnel vision as she had accused Nathan of being.

She was going to have to ask his forgiveness and for a second chance. She could only hope he would want to try again. Even though he said he loved her, she had been so careless with that love that she wouldn't blame him if he ran in the opposite direction when he saw her coming.

What a jumbled-up, hopeless mess. What was she going to do? Almost automatically she turned her car toward the person she had always run to when she was hurt.

She found Eugenia curled up with a murder mystery. After one glance at Liz's face, the older woman put down her book.

"I've been acting like seven hundred different kinds of fools," Liz said, sitting down beside her.

"After all you said today, I knew you'd be back." Eugenia shook her head. "But I hope you didn't come here looking for sympathy. Because I don't have any for you."

Ten

Spring had played a trick on Nashville, Nathan decided as he peered out the window. A cold, misting rain had replaced yesterday's sunshine. He thought the gloom seemed rather appropriate.

"Mr. Summerfield?"

At the sound of the secretary's voice, Nathan turned from the window. She was addressing the man seated at the head of the long, glass-topped conference table.

"They're here," she said as if announcing a royal entourage. The man stood. The other two men at the table followed suit. Nathan stepped forward.

Liz was the first person through the door. The only person as far as Nathan was concerned. She was wearing the same gray suit she had worn the day he had watched her in court. The same jaunty red handkerchief was tucked into the front pocket. But when he looked into her eyes, he didn't see the usual confidence. Her expression was uncertain and maybe a little wistful.

"Mr. Hollister?" When the sound of his name penetrated his absorption in Liz, Nathan realized it had probably been called more than once.

"Sorry," he murmured sheepishly and took his seat beside Claxton Summerfield. He found himself directly across from Liz. He could even smell her perfume. Looking away from her, he thought of the door he had slammed last night. It was too bad he had to wait until after this meeting to find out if the other closed doors between them had any chance of opening.

While introductions were made around the table, Liz tried not to be obvious in her study of Nathan. He looked tired and pale. His hair was unruly, as if he'd hurried through the rain. It always curled like that when he didn't comb it right after showering. She had teased him about it more than once.

"Shall we begin?"

Summerfield's booming voice jerked her back to the present, and she realized she had barely glanced at the man she had been hoping to meet for so long. He was younger than she had expected—perhaps only in his early to mid-forties. He looked fit, with the ruddy complexion of an outdoorsman and auburn hair brushed with gray at his temples. The only feature of his that fit her preconceived notions was the shrewd, nononsense gleam in the brown-eyed gaze he lifted to hers.

A formidable opponent, she decided, and prepared to do battle.

Formidable but fair, she had to amend a few minutes later.

Summerfield had agreed to almost all of their demands. The most pressing repairs would be made right away. For the others, he would supply the materials, and as set forth in their original proposal, the tenants would provide the labor. Furthermore, he promised a response time of no less than twenty-four hours in the event of any situation—such as a broken staircase rail—that posed an immediate threat to anyone's safety. The tenant association's board members agreed without argument. It was wrapped up that fast. That easily.

"I want to express my apologies for the way this entire matter has been handled," Summerfield said. "Especially in regard to the conduct of my associate, Mr. Eldon Rogers. He's no longer in my employ."

Liz slanted a surprised glance in Nathan's direction. He was already pushing away from the table.

"If it wouldn't be an inconvenience," he said, addressing the tenants as he stood. "There are a couple of members of the media waiting outside. Your demonstration yesterday caused a sensation of sorts, and Mr. Summerfield would be grateful if you'd agree to answer their questions, to tell them how you feel about the agreement that's been reached." His gaze slid to Liz's. "If you don't want to talk with them, we'll take you out the back door. It's up to you."

"It sounds okay to me," the president agreed, looking to Liz for confirmation.

She shrugged. "Your decision."

In minutes the room was filled with reporters. The news of Summerfield's expected candidacy must have leaked, Liz thought as she prepared to navigate around the edge of the crowd to the door. It was over a year until the primaries, but there was something to be said for being the first out of the gate.

"Miss Patterson?"

She turned to find Summerfield himself bearing down on her. "Is there something else, sir?"

"Only this." He put out his hand. "I think I owe you at least that much for looking out for my business. It's certainly more than I was doing myself. Thank you."

His handshake was firm. Perfect for a politician, she decided, suppressing a smile. "Just live up to your agreement. That's all the thanks I need."

"You got it." With a final press of her fingers, he turned to answer a reporter's question.

Waving a goodbye to her friends, Liz headed for the door again. This time it was Nathan who intercepted her.

"Wanna blow this joint?" He was smiling, hazel eyes crinkling at the corners. Only someone who knew him as well as Liz would notice the fine edge of wariness in his posture.

"Don't you have a job to do?" she asked.

He nodded to an attractive blonde who was standing at Summerfield's side. "My assistant needs a trial by fire, and there's no time like the present." He took Liz's hand. "Come on."

"Nathan, we're in a strange person's office," Liz protested after he had lead her down a corridor and through the first open door. "And I'll bet it's Summerfield's office," she added, turning around in the center of a large, corner room with leather-upholstered furniture and an expansive view of the city. Nathan turned the lock on the door.

"What if he needs to get in here?" she asked. How could Nathan act so normal when they had been screaming at each other last night, when she had treated him so badly?

"He owes you a favor or two." Nathan perched casually on the edge of the desk, as if it belonged to him. "Besides, don't you want to hear about 'ol Eldon Rogers?"

The last thing Liz wanted to discuss was Rogers. *What about you and me?* she wanted to say. But she didn't. Instead she put her briefcase down on a chair and forced her voice to stay light as she said, "Don't tell me—Summerfield fired him because he was a jerk?"

"And a thief," Nathan replied bluntly. "Rogers has been in charge of those apartment buildings for five years, and he's been skimming money from the revenues from the beginning. He confessed to everything this morning. The manager who was attacked was in on it with him. That's why he liked getting the rent in cash. You ought to impress upon your pals the benefits of paying by check."

"Didn't Summerfield think something odd was going on when the manager was beaten up and his company paid all of Marissa Lockhart's medical bills?"

"Rogers was able to hide it."

Liz shook her head in disbelief. "So you were right. Summerfield wasn't the villain at all. I should have listened to you last night."

"I believe there are some things about yesterday we both would do differently if we had the chance." Nathan's voice was quiet, his expression so intense Liz turned away.

"Summerfield certainly runs a loose ship," she murmured. "What does that say about his qualifications for Senator?"

"Hey," Nathan said. "He's a busy man. Give him a break. Those apartment buildings are a small part of his holdings. Rogers has worked for Summerfield for fifteen years and for his father before that. There was no reason not to trust him."

Liz looked at him again and stepped closer. "Busy men can lose track of important details."

"Help me make sure I don't do that," Nathan murmured as he caught her hand in his. He pulled her to him. The trepidation was gone from his eyes. "Can you believe me when I tell you I know what's most important in my life?"

She raised her hand to his face. It was so handsome, but even if it weren't, it would still be so very dear to her. "I'll accept that you've got your priorities in line, but only if you'll believe me when I tell you how sorry I am for the way I've acted."

"Well," he admitted, flashing his smile. "You don't cut a man much slack, Miss Patterson."

"What a perfectly diplomatic public relations-type answer," she murmured, grinning. Then she sobered. "I've been acting like an inflexible little hypocrite, and that's a direct quote from Eugenia."

"Not a hypocrite," Nathan replied.

"How about just inflexible then? Or unyielding? Judgmental? I believe she used all of those adjectives in putting me in my place last night." Liz ran her fingers beneath the lapels of his navy jacket and concentrated on the stripes in his tie. If she looked at him, she'd lose track of everything she wanted to say. "But for everything she called me, I called myself something worse. I've been expecting you to do all the changing, all the giving. I haven't tried to do anything to accommodate you. I wouldn't even listen to you last night when you tried to tell me about Summerfield." She finally tilted her head back again. "I wouldn't blame you if you had decided I didn't deserve to be loved."

"Oh, no. There's no chance of that." Nathan lowered his mouth to hers, kissing her with all the pent-up yearning and frustration of the last few days. More than anything, he had missed the taste of her, he decided, the sweetness of her lips. His hands slid up to her softer-than-silk hair, destroying her carefully arranged bun.

Laughing, she drew away and shook her head. The chestnut strands tumbled about her shoulders.

"I love you," Nathan said fiercely, framing her vibrant face between his hands. "But I can't promise you it's going to be easy. I know I'm still going to make you angry."

"I don't think I could love you if you didn't."

His hands moved to her shoulders. "I'm serious. I can be a selfish pig."

"I knew that from the start."

"But I'll never do anything to hurt you, Liz. Never. Nothing is ever going to come between us again. Not my business—"

"Not my causes, either," she promised.

"How about if we just try to support each other, respect each other's differences?"

"A very sensible plan."

"You know what? I could attain each and every one of my goals, and it wouldn't mean anything to me if I don't have you." He kissed her again.

Liz pulled back. "I guess that's a pretty heavy-duty statement for the original self-involved guy."

"Anyone can change with the right incentive."

Her breath actually caught at the look in his eyes. "I love you, Nathan."

"And do you still think love's not enough?"

"It is when you add some trust." She pressed her lips to his chin. "And some respect." Her mouth moved over his, lightly. "And some patience."

"More of Eugenia's words of wisdom?" His mouth opened beneath hers before she could answer. "That Eugenia's some smart old bird," he murmured moments later.

"And she'd better never hear you call her that."

"Wouldn't she forgive a close relative?"

"Maybe."

"Then marry me," Nathan whispered. "I'd like to be part of the family."

"You haven't met my parents yet. You might change your mind."

"Not a chance." His lips captured hers again. His hands skimmed down her body, the sides of her breasts, the outer edge of her hips.

Liz's reaction was the same as it had been the first time he touched her. She shivered from the heat. "Promise me," she said. "Promise me that even after we're married for fifty years, it'll still feel like magic when you do that."

"I'll try. That's all I can promise."

"Then it's good enough for me."

He grinned mischievously. "You need to promise me something, too."

"Anything."

"A vote for Summerfield. I need the support."

Liz giggled. "Well, I don't know that he shares my ideological point of view. But—" she slipped her hands under his jacket "—you could do some serious campaigning. It's early yet. My vote could be won."

"I'll do my best," he murmured, bending his head toward hers. But before they could kiss, the doorknob was turned, then a knock sounded at the door, followed by Summerfield's angry voice demanding to know what was going on.

Nathan rolled his eyes heavenward. "If his timing stays this rotten, I may not vote for him myself."

Eugenia paused midway down the staircase, struck by the perfection of the sights and sounds below her. The foyer was filled with music and laughter and the whirling colors of couples dancing. Finally, she thought, people are really dancing again, the way it was meant to be done.

The scene could have been a picture cut from her own youth. Taken when the doors of this big old house had opened wide to receive her friends, the days when she was the life of any party.

But this wasn't her day or her party. It belonged to Liz. And to Nathan.

And how happy that made her sentimental old heart.

They were at the center of the dancing crowd. Against his black tuxedo jacket, her white satin dress swirled like snow against an evening sky. Such a contrast they were. But so complementary.

Eugenia smiled in approval as Liz's diamond earrings caught the light from the chandelier. They matched the sparkle in Liz's eyes when she looked at her groom.

Eugenia turned as Jeannette came to stand beside her.

"Our Liz is happy. Right, *madame*?"

Smiling at her old friend, Eugenia nodded. "Yes, very happy."

"But the others." Jeannette shook her head sadly. "What are we to do?"

Frowning, Eugenia glanced back to the crowd. Sure enough, Maggie was sidelined with that insufferable bore named Don. Cassandra was dancing, but not with the person Eugenia was certain she belonged with. She sighed. "I guess our work is never done, Jeannette, never done."

But before she rejoined the party and took up her self-appointed tasks, Eugenia paused for a moment more on the stairs. She looked at Nathan and Liz, and she let the music take her back. To another night. In another age. To the scent of flowers and the touch of one man's lips.

To have known romance, she thought, oh, but that made one whole.

* * * * *

Aunt Eugenia strikes again! And this time it's fiery, passionate Cassandra who's the subject of her matchmaking schemes. RUBY FIRE is a sizzling story of growing up and falling in love. Watch for it in February 1990 from Silhouette Desire.

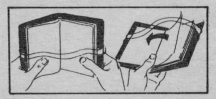

SILHOUETTE DESIRE™

presents

AUNT EUGENIA'S TREASURES
by CELESTE HAMILTON

Liz, Cassandra and Maggie are the honored recipients of Aunt Eugenia's heirloom jewels...but Eugenia knows the real prizes are the young women themselves. Read about Aunt Eugenia's quest to find them everlasting love. Each book shines on its own, but together, they're priceless!

Available in December:
THE DIAMOND'S SPARKLE (SD #537)

Altruistic Liz Patterson wants nothing to do with Nathan Hollister, but as the fast-lane PR man tells Liz, love is something he's willing to take *very* slowly.

Available in February:
RUBY FIRE (SD #549)

Impulsive Cassandra Martin returns from her travels... ready to rekindle the flame with the man she never forgot, Daniel O'Grady.

Available in April:
THE HIDDEN PEARL (SD #561)

Cautious Maggie O'Grady comes out of her shell...and glows in the precious warmth of love when brazen Jonah Pendleton moves in next door.

Wonderful, luxurious gifts can be yours with proofs-of-purchase from any specially marked "Indulge A Little" Harlequin or Silhouette book with the Offer Certificate properly completed, plus a check or money order (do not send cash) to cover postage and handling payable to Harlequin/Silhouette "Indulge A Little, Give A Lot" Offer. We will send you the specified gift.

Mail-in-Offer

OFFER CERTIFICATE

Item:	A. Collector's Doll	B. Soaps in a Basket	C. Potpourri Sachet	D. Scented Hangers
# of Proofs-of-Purchase	18	12	6	4
Postage & Handling	$3.25	$2.75	$2.25	$2.00
Check One				

Name _____

Address _____ Apt. # _____

City _____ State _____ Zip _____

ONE PROOF OF PURCHASE

To collect your free gift by mail you must include the necessary number of proofs-of-purchase plus postage and handling with offer certificate.

SD-3

Harlequin®/Silhouette®

Mail this certificate, designated number of proofs-of-purchase and check or money order for postage and handling to:

INDULGE A LITTLE
P.O. Box 9055
Buffalo, N.Y. 14269-9055